FLAME KISSED

PHOENIX RISING BOOK ONE

ANNIE ANDERSON

FLAME KISSED
Phoenix Rising Book One
Annie Anderson
Published by Annie Anderson
Copyright © 2015 Annie Anderson
Edited by: Angela Sanders
Cover Art by: Tattered Quill Designs
All rights reserved.
Paperback ISBN: 978-1-960315-20-5

This book is dedicated to my husband.
Babe, thank you for being awesome enough to inspire a
leading man based on your hotness.
Love you.

PROLOGUE

AURELIA—1855

FATES, HELP ME. THEY ARE GOING TO KILL EACH OTHER.

Breath saws through my lungs as I whip my head, searching. The colors of the withering leaves tumble and writhe together as I stumble through the forest. I can't see them, but I know they're out there. Just like I know something is wrong.

I can't find him. I can't. I can't.

But what's more, I don't *want* to find him—or rather *them*. I do not want to see another reality of a vision I will never change. I don't want to confirm the truth that is painfully etching its way into my soul.

Dead leaves crunch beneath my feet as I scramble

through the bedrock and crest the first foothill toward the outlook cliff.

Stupid skirt. Stupid slippery shoes.

I'm not moving quickly enough, but in my state, I'm surprised I can move at all. Cradling the swell of my belly, I try to climb faster, the stitch in my side nearly bringing me to my knees.

Where are they?

I stop and search the sky for them—for their flames, for their wings, but I know it's too late. It is rapidly darkening to the inky black of evening of the early Autumn, and without the light from the moon tonight, I'll never see as properly as I should.

A vision slams into my consciousness once more: my husband and his childhood friend, Rhys, locked in the heat of battle. I want to shout, but I'm lost to the depths of their conflict, and as my husband rains down a blow upon his friend, my eyes snap open. I'm overcome with disillusion at first, the phantom pains from the vision ripping through my flesh. Then I see the very real blood dripping down my arm.

But I'm alone. How can this be happening?

I hear and see no one, only the large gaping gash that has torn open my arm from wrist to elbow. The coppery bite of blood turns my stomach as the warm, sticky stream seeps past my fingers and drips onto the dirt.

Blackness clouds my vision for a moment, but I force myself to forget the constant pulse of my injury and pull myself together. Ripping a swath from my billowing skirt, I use the fabric to bind my arm in an effort to stem the bleeding. The navy-blue patterned fabric turns indigo from the blood quickly oozing from my wound.

I should already be healing, but I'm not.

Dread fills my gut as the nausea returns.

This is not good.

Picking myself up from the gritty forest floor, I rethink the panicked pace of before and plod forward at a more sedate pace. Running with this injury just isn't possible. I'm already pushing it with this silly corset and dress, especially in my delicate condition.

As if impending motherhood was anything but delicate.

There.

The sound of Rhys and Lucien clashing together somewhere in the distance rings through my ears. If I don't get there in time, I am certain they'll kill each other. The chilling growl of an angry man drifts through the trees, and my feet carry me faster as if they have a mind of their own.

But when I get there, I realize I should never have stopped to catch my breath.

I should never have bound my wound.

I shouldn't have waited.

"Lucien?" The whisper of his name falls from my lips on a sob.

My husband is on the ground, and all it takes is one look at his still form to know he's dead. I know, just as I knew I was with child long before my cycle refused to come. How I knew so many things that I wished I didn't.

"Lucien?"

His cool blue eyes fail to move. They simply stare at the rapidly darkening sky, his body still and cold.

Lucien's not breathing, and Rhys is just standing there bleeding, holding the blade he used to kill my husband. Holding that same blasted knife that I saw in my vision.

No. No. No.

I haven't a clue as to what made me do it. And looking back, it's still a mystery to me as to how the blade moved from Rhys' loose grip and into my hand, or how exactly I knew where to pierce his flesh to hurt him the most.

Driving the blade home in his flesh, blood instantly pours from my own belly, down my bodice, and through my skirt. Shock and bitter anguish tears through me as realization dawns.

I knew then that when my arm had been sliced, it had actually been Rhys who had gotten cut first—it had been Rhys who had bled first.

I stabbed him, but we both bled.

Bound, my mind screams. *We are bound.*

Then the contractions start.

And I will forever blame Rhys for two deaths that day.

I

AURELIA

It starts just like they always do, from the blackness of a sleep so deep, the fabric of what is real and what is dream weaves together to make what would be.

An entryway or vestibule, the room seemed small. A little girl had opened the door, a lovely walnut wood, inlaid with a stained-glass window. The mother's heels clicked against the cream-colored marble floor with an urgent gait as she hurried toward her daughter, her pink skirt suit swishing against her legs as she fiddled with the simple strand of understated pearls at her neck.

"I thought I told you not to—"

The girl's white-blonde hair practically gleamed against her skin as her mouth formed an "O" of surprise. She was young, maybe six or seven, and deeply tan, as only children could be with their terminable immunity to the heat and sun.

Moving behind the girl, the shock on the mother's face morphed into fear so quickly her features seemed to warp, like a piece of untreated wood that had been left to the elements to rot.

She gripped her daughter's shoulders, shaking her violently in an attempt to get the poor girl to move, to back away from the looming shadow. Clearly male, the figure was backlit by the rising sun. The woman recognized the man, however. She didn't need to see his face to know what danger lay before them—she could easily see the large caliber handgun gripped in his meaty palm.

Shrieking for her daughter to run, the mother roughly tugged the poor girl behind her back. But her daughter was either in shock or too scared to move because she stayed rooted to the spot, clutching the hem of her mother's designer suit.

Slowly, calmly, the man raised his gun as if he had all the time in the world to take his shot. The muzzle fired once, and a tiny hole appeared in the woman's chest. A small trickle of blood bloomed over the heart of her blouse. She went down slowly, dropping first to her knees, sliding to her bottom, and then to her side. Even in death, she was careful not to fall on her child. Again, the muzzle fired, and this time, the daughter collapsed, her wound considerably less pretty, given the caliber of the gun and her small size.

And in that tiny little vestibule, in what was surely a beautiful home of a nice family, the mother and daughter were left to cool in their drying lifeblood.

I SHOULD WAKE UP SCREAMING, BUT I DON'T. AFTER THESE many years, dreaming night after night of the horrors people inflict on one another, I stopped screaming several decades ago. As per usual, though, I sit bolt upright in my bed, sheets tangled around my legs, damp with cold sweat.

My best friend Evan would call me a psychic, but I tell her on the regular she's full of shit. Psychics know things before they happen, and I do. On occasion.

But not enough for me to actually make a difference.

Not enough to save the people who need saving.

And just once? I'd really like to be wrong.

For curiosity's sake, I pull my laptop onto the bed, praying I don't blow up this beautiful piece of equipment. I have a bad habit of frying electrical devices when I'm upset, and watching a mom and daughter get gunned down in their home definitely puts me in the "agitated" column. In fact, this is my fourth laptop this year.

Closing my eyes, I take a deep breath. Once marginally centered, I type the local news site into the browser. Sure enough, the breaking news story is of Victoria Ness, thirty-four, and Vivian Ness, seven, who were gunned down in their University Park home two hours ago. The shooter, Victoria's estranged husband, then turned the gun on himself.

Figures.

What kind of psychic am I? Well, evidently, I'm the shitty kind. I *maybe* see ten percent of what I should, and I can't alter a single second of it. I see what I see, and then I brace myself because it's going to happen. There's nothing I can do.

Believe me, I've tried.

Just once I'd like to have a vision I could change.

Just once I'd like to see something other than how *and* when someone will die.

But I know my fate, and sanity just isn't in the cards for me.

Staring out the huge picture window, I take in the view of the mountain range beyond. The craggy rocks and giant boulders are so vastly different from where I started my life. There are fewer trees here in the subalpine Rockies than in the Pacific Northwest, and the sun shines more days throughout the year. The heat, the sun, the smell of dry earth—all these differences help me breathe when I wake from a new vision.

A new death.

Seeing that blue sky goes a long way to calm me down when I should be rocking in a corner.

Getting out of bed, I immediately rip off the sweat-soaked sheets. It's a ritual of sorts. A fresh start. A means of washing away a death I can't change, and the helplessness of another life gone. Snapping the clean sheets on the bed, I begin bracing myself for the total freaking production tonight will be.

I have an art show this evening, and though it's July in Denver, I'll be covered from neck to ankles to hide the ink on my skin, wear contacts to cloak the eyes that mark me as what I am, and pray that no one finds me. Yes, it's Denver, and yes, even grandmothers are inked these days, but it's the eyes that get people.

As a seer, I was born with the ability to observe events that will come to pass in vivid Technicolor right inside my little noggin. And my eyes? They marked me before I ever had my first vision. My irises are an extraordinarily pale, milky green. Like in old westerns where the elderly guy is blind, and he has those freaky eyes where the iris and pupil nearly blend into the sclera? Yep, that's what I've got going on here.

But my sight is better than most humans. Likely better than most Ethereals, too. But the Ethereal community prefers not to remember we even exist—our presence reminding them that there's no such thing as a true immortal. Everything dies. Witch or warlock, wraith, or even a meager human, they all perish in the end. And when they do, flames and wings are what you better hope you see.

It's better than the alternative.

And let's not get into the fact that sometimes I randomly electrocute people without meaning to. If people weren't already looking at me funny before—*which they are, because my eyes freak people way the hell out*—they would after I randomly zapped them.

So I wear contacts when I leave my home, because if I don't, people assume I'm blind, for one, and they act all awkward and try to help me do stuff or get around. Or *numero dos*: their faces say they are skeeved way the hell out. Also, when I'm pissed, they kind of, well, glow.

Like an incandescent bulb, *glow*.

So the fact that I'm different is really fucking obvious and that doesn't even touch on the flames.

Or the wings.

Hello, my name is Aurelia Constantine, and I am a phoenix.

No offense to Greek mythology, but I'm not a damn

bird. I'm a person. I just so happen—on occasion—to burst into flames, have visions, and electrocute people with a shield that I can't seem to control. Oh, and those wings? Very, very real.

And they're persnickety little bitches to boot.

My last phase totally ruined my favorite leather jacket. I've had that jacket for the past twenty years. They just don't make leather like they used to. Replacing it was a pain in the ass, and in the end, I had to have it custom made.

Also, I don't age. Or die. Wait. I take that back. I've died. *A lot.* I just don't *stay* dead.

I've looked thirty-ish for the last one hundred and fifty years or so. Since I was born about thirty years prior to the aging halt, I'm assuming my kind ages at a normal rate until we reach our bodies' maturity. Then we stop aging altogether.

Or it could just be me.

I *should* know all these details for sure, *should* be knowledgeable about the basic facets of my species, but escaping my Legion at twenty means I was never taught several important aspects of being what I am.

What I do know is that when you're a seer in my culture and reach maturity, you get permanently blinded so your visions will be "pure"—whatever the hell that means—transforming a lowly seer into an oracle.

Our visions are important. Seers and oracles alike foresee visions of death, and in predicting death, we can direct the gentry to the dead or dying to send the souls on to be reborn. Seers cannot change the outcome of their visions. Oracles, however, have enough advanced warning and the power to change the future.

In my mind, it is the only advantage for the price they paid when they gave away their eyes.

One hundred and eighty years I've been alive, and for nearly all of them, I've been running. Hiding amongst the humans so ignorant of our existence. Trying so hard to blend in, not get caught again by the people I once called family. Doing my best to make sure I don't lose what little autonomy I have left.

But all it takes is one person to put two and two together and realize I'm not human.

All it takes is one person to notice my differences or see me change into what I really am.

All it takes is one person to remember me, and I'll be fucked.

Truth be told, I'd prefer not to go to the show at all and just get the check for any of my work that's sold. I'd rather change into fresh pajamas, order takeout, and binge *Supernatural* for the five-zillionth time. But Evan, who does double duty as the curator for the James Gallery and the poor soul who calls herself my best friend, has decided I'm a shut-in long enough three hundred or so days a year.

Every single opening, she makes me go and pretend to look at my art like a real live person, who breathes and speaks and shit. It's utterly exhausting. Personally, I think she's overexaggerating. I go out. Occasionally. To get tattoos and groceries—but so what? That counts as out, dammit.

Why she's my friend, I'll never know.

I say that, but I know why. She's my friend, because when I was at my lowest, when I thought I couldn't go on another day, she crashed into my life and gave me someone to look after. She is the yin to my yang, the Disco to my Heavy Metal.

In reality, she's a wraith princess, the only child of John Black, the Wraith King. Phoenixes and wraiths are supposed to hate each other, but I couldn't hate that girl if someone paid me. Other wraiths are a bit sketchy, but Evan, she is the light in the darkness.

I just wish she'd let me stay home and avoid this whole mess.

So far, I've managed to maintain my anonymity. That's what Evan is for—because she can be in the spotlight when I can't. She has the freedom to move from city to city, selling, curating, being an all-around wonderkid where I cannot.

All because of my stupid Legion.

So tonight, I'll be hiding in plain sight, eating finger food and drinking cheap wine like any other art-consuming hipster, pretending I'm not the one who painted the pretty pictures.

Suddenly, "Shake Your Groove Thing" blasts from the speakers of my phone. Why Evan thought Peaches & Herb was an appropriate ringtone, I'll never know.

"What?" I answer, knowing she is T-minus three seconds from an Opening Day meltdown of Chernobyl proportions.

"Where in the blue fuck are you? You were supposed to be down the mountain already and driving into Denver, and your ass is probably still sitting in bed! You do this to me *every* single *time*. Dammit, *Ari*, get your *ass* in gear."

"I'm getting a very bad feeling about tonight," I whisper, but I say this each and every time.

This time, though, it's the whisper that catches her attention.

"You see anything?" she breathes.

Evan knows too much. Well, Evan knows pretty much everything. I know she feeds most of the information to Rhys, but I can't muster up the courage to tell her to stop. Evan is like a dog with a bone.

"Nothing but a murder this morning. You know the Ness family?"

"Yeah, I do," is all that comes through the line on a broken gasp. "They're huge patrons. They're supposed to be here tonight."

A bone-deep chill races down the length of my spine.

Houston, we have a problem.

"Well, they're not coming. I don't think I am, either."

"We've been through this." She sighs heavily. "You *have* to be here, Ari. You have to see how your work affects people, how it moves them. If anything, I'm begging you to be here for me. Victoria was a friend."

I feel horrible. I'm sad for that family, but only on the periphery. Evan actually knew her.

"I don't have to do anything. Especially since you've been ditching our sparring sessions and avoiding me for the last month."

"But—"

"But, I will...for you. Give me ten and I'll be heading down the mountain."

"Thank you." The relief in her voice hits me square in the chest.

"Yeah, yeah. Don't make me regret it," I say with a roll of my eyes she can't see. "There better be yummy snacks."

"Of *course* there'll be yummy snacks. What kind of operation do you think I'm running here? I have to give the patrons *something* since the artist is conspicuously missing. Again," Evan huffs. "The things I do for you."

"Snacks."

"Yeah, yeah. I got your snacks."

"Thanks. See you in forty-five."

Ending the call, I rush through the disguise prep, but instead of the dowdy outfit I was planning on, I opt to dress in attire that will be easier to fight in. In lieu of the brown suit, whose added fabric will hinder my movement and ease of weapon retrieval, I pick a nice pair of fitted black straight-legged slacks with a good, thick heft to them. I pair it with the matching jacket that helps conceal my tattoos and spine holster.

I choose a blousy, sapphire peplum top to go under the jacket (because I'm a freaking girl and I need the pretty). In the same vein, I pick my black leather, four-inch wedge-heeled booties with the weapon loops sewn into the inner lining. One would think I couldn't run, fight, or walk in these beauties, but they'd be wrong. These are the most comfortable pair of shoes I own, and likely, they're the most functional.

Shakily, I still put in the emerald-green contacts, put my hair in a bun at the back of my head, and throw in a few stainless-steel spikes as hair sticks. I love them because they are as thin as knitting needles, sharp as knives, and hide in plain sight.

Just in case the shiver of fear I feel is the real thing, I slide three thin throwing knives in the holder in my right bootie, and load and stow a Glock 19 in the specialty-made left-handed spine holster.

And Evan wonders why I don't go outside. Wearing enough weapons to satisfy me is a production and a half.

As I head out to the garage, a cool finger of dread prickles at the base of my neck. Just in case, I step back inside and carefully open the gun cabinet disguised as a full-length mirror. Picking up a few extra mags, I stow them in the ammo loops of my left bootie.

Ready as I'll ever be.

Let's just hope I don't die again.

2

AURELIA

Screeching into my parking spot at the gallery, I turn the car off and hop out of the seat like my ass is on fire. I'm late—just as Evan predicted I would be—which is irritating. Somehow, despite my abilities, I still managed to get caught in traffic. Which is just par for the freaking course in my book.

Of course, I have about the worst ability on the planet that only seems to work in fits and spurts.

Did I know I would get caught in traffic? Technically, yes, but I thought I could go around it, having no idea that even the side roads would be backed up, too. Did I know that Rhys was four cars behind me the whole way down the mountain and parked on the street to avoid me spotting him? Yes, I did. I also know he has on mismatched socks and a Morganite knife in his boot.

But none of that information is useful, and all I'm stuck with is a feeling in my gut that I didn't pack enough weapons.

Slipping in the hidden side entrance, I try to skirt the crowd without being noticed as I make my way to the only reason I'm here.

Food.

Assessing the spread on the snack table, I mentally give Evan kudos. Cubed cheeses, grapes, bruschetta, those cute little cucumber chive cups, pancetta cheese tomato skewers, and a bunch of other yummy snacks decorate one massive table positioned expertly next to the open bar.

I have to give it to her. The little devil really knows how to throw a party.

Speaking of the devil, Evan pops up by my side as if she materialized from thin air. Which isn't too far from what she's actually capable of. The jury's still out on whether she just showed up on her own two feet, or if she appeared in a puff of smoke in front of an entire roomful of people. I'm going with option one solely based on the number of humans in the room.

While it's great my showing is well attended, the room is far too people-y for me. But the crowd isn't the only thing giving me pause. Despite the riot of curls and tiny stature, my pixie of a best friend is typically a little more robust than she is right now. And while I feed her until she busts every time she comes over, I have a feeling she isn't getting sustenance from the other half of her diet—the soul-eating side.

It's not as bad as it sounds. As a wraith, Evan eats damned souls, transporting them on a one-way slide straight to Hell. By the sharpness to her cheekbones, she hasn't consumed a soul in a hot minute.

I want to ask her about it, but this is neither the time nor the place.

"Finally decided to grace us with your presence?" Evan asks with a snarky little smile. "I thought I was going to have to send out a search party. And by search party, I mean your personal guard dog."

Rude. After a century-plus of us being BFFs, Evan has tried to get me to forgive Rhys about three billion and one times. She would love to lock us in a room together and throw away the key. I'd likely end up killing him, which would temporarily end up killing both of us. Wouldn't be the first time.

Phoenix bondings are stupid.

I hate that I wonder if he's okay. I loathe that I worry that he's not happy, if he's in the same Hell as I am. If he regrets what happened to us. But more? I hate that the bond makes me care at all—makes me want to give in to the love of a man I should detest.

Picking up a plate, I slide a few of the cucumber cups onto it before moving to the pancetta.

"Below the belt, Evangeline," I mutter, sending her a healthy dose of side-eye. "Give me time to inhale some of these goodies before you start in on me."

Using her given name makes her eye twitch, which was the intended goal. If she's going to hit me where it hurts, I'll do the same to her. She purses her red-painted lips, undoubtedly deciding if yelling at me in this room full of people would be worth the ass-kicking she'd get later.

"You've sold four already," she offers, diverting from the thorny Rhys talk. "Simone is wheedling with two others for the dollhouse painting. I think that one is going to start a bidding war in a minute."

Nodding, I stuff a morsel in my mouth—whole— and chew. I don't really care how much the paintings sell for—I only want them gone. All of them—every single one—is a depiction of how someone died, an artistic rendering of the deaths that stayed with me long after I opened my eyes. The dollhouse is my least favorite, and I'll be glad to see it go.

"Here," she says, offering me a small cut crystal whiskey glass.

Gratefully, I accept it and take a healthy swig, allowing the burn of the alcohol to warm me. Yeah, it's July, but staring at these paintings make me shiver.

Suddenly, I yank Evan behind the cover of a steel column, pushing her little body in between the edges of the I-beam, unable to articulate the pictures that just rolled across my brain in enough time.

"What—" Evan squawks before the *ping-ping-ping* of bullets hit the metal.

Screams erupt around us, the crowd stampeding to the exits, and I wonder if I have enough cover to get Evan behind the snack table.

"When I say 'go,' you flip that table over and get behind it," I order, staring Evan down.

She nods, pressing her lips together so hard they turn white around the edges.

The images in my brain tell me there are two phoenixes—soldiers to be exact. Great. I slide out from the cover of the I-beam, pull the gun from my spine holster, and yell for Evan to go, before the soldier in front of me even has time to blink. Wasting five shots on his vest, I quickly realize he's wearing body armor before he starts returning fire.

Taking off into a run, I move in between two freestanding walls that wouldn't stop a BB gun, and keep moving to the next I-beam. But I can't stay here much longer. The other soldier skirts around the periphery of the room, ready to corner me. I'm being herded.

Fantastic.

Moans of pain reach my ears, and it's all I can do to swallow down my tears as I attempt to block them out. Focusing on the heavy footfalls, I try to gauge their position. Reaching up, I pull one of my hair sticks from the bun and throw it like a missile. I enjoy the girly scream coming from a man's mouth—more than I can possibly say—as the thin rod of metal embeds into his eye. Grabbing three more, I toss a few into the shoulder of his compatriot before giving him a matching skewer in his other eye.

Above everything—the moans of pain from patrons caught in the crossfire, the sound of a gun being reloaded, the screeching of the phoenix who'll have to regrow his eyes—I hear the whimpers of my best friend.

Shit.

Evan is softer than I am, and not that she can't handle herself—she can—but she hasn't seen the things I have. She hasn't endured. And she can't be around the death coming for us without phasing—something she shouldn't ever do in public.

If I phase, I look like an angel. Evan, however, resembles something out of a nightmare.

Avoiding the perimeter of the room, I manage to circle back to her, practically doing a baseball slide to dodge the bullets aimed for my head as I make it back to cover. After a second of inspection, I realize all too quickly from the hallmarks of blackened eyes and inch-long fangs that Evan is about a nanosecond from losing it.

"Get out of here," I insist, reloading my Glock as I desperately try not to succumb to the fire that begs to explode from my skin.

My best friend isn't like other wraiths, and that fact is made all too apparent when pieces of the floor start abrading away beneath her. I've seen her level an entire city once—by accident—over a century ago. Granted, her control has grown exponentially since then, but I'm not eager to push it.

Evangeline doesn't acknowledge me at all, lost in bloodlust or fear or something I can't name. Despite my unwillingness to hurt her, I can't have a repeat of San Francisco. My free hand cracks across her face, and the inky quality to her wraith eyes slowly bleed back to human.

She sucks in a breath, shaking herself back to sanity.

"Get out of here," I repeat, growling so she knows I mean business.

She scrambles backward, still under cover of the table, cowering at the barest edge. Her fear for me burns, even as necessary as it might be.

"What about you?" she croaks, still worried about me even though I just slapped her.

Her voice shakes even through her fangs as she tries to keep herself in check.

"Rhys is here somewhere. He'll back me up once he finally sacks up and gets out of his truck. I'll be fine. Meet you at the cabin?"

Evan takes two deep breaths, one after the other, before she gives me a hesitant nod.

"Good. Get the hell out of here so I can kill these idiots. Say hi to the parental units for me."

Evan smiles hesitantly before a swirl of black smoke envelopes her and she disappears, traveling to her family's cabin in Grand Lake. Now all I need to do is take out the trash...

What I didn't tell her was that Rhys likely won't get out of his truck. He most likely won't come in at all, and depending on where he parked, he might not see the stream of people flooding out of here like their hair is on fire or hear the shots from these idiots' hand cannons.

That's on me, I suppose. I've made it clear over the last century and a half that I don't want to see him, and I don't need his help. Typically, I don't, and today is probably no different.

Maybe.

I'm pretty sure I can take care of these two jokers on my own, but what if they aren't alone?

What if this is it? What if these are my last free breaths?

A guttural gasp breaks into my thoughts, and I shrug out of my jacket. A man not ten feet from me has a bullet in his gut. I try to keep my eyes closed as the vision of his death on an operating table fills my mind, little details about the man coming with it. I didn't need a vision to tell me he was a goner, but I lay down cover fire as I sneak out of my hidey-hole to drag him to the modicum of safety the table provides.

Pressing my jacket to his wound, I whisper, "Everything is going to be all right, George. Don't you worry. Keep pressure on that, okay? Help is coming."

It's a lie, but he doesn't need to know that. All George wanted was to buy a little art for his college-aged daughter. He didn't ask to be gunned down in the middle of an art show.

A burning-hot prickle to my skin has me sucking in deep breaths for calm. The absolute last thing this poor man needs to see in his final moments is me turning into a smoldering Valkyrie.

He needs vengeance.

And he'll get it as soon as Rhys removes his head from his ass and gets in here.

Whenever that will be.

3

RHYS

GUILT IS SOMETHING I LIVE WITH ON A DAILY BASIS, BUT IT gets worse on days like today. Today I get to play stalker to a woman I've been in love with every single day for the last century and a half.

A woman I cannot have.

A woman who hates me with every single fiber of her being.

Go me.

As her soldier, I've been bound to Aurelia for nearly one hundred and sixty years. I thought as a young man I knew what love was. The inane notion I assumed was love as a boy is nothing compared to the iron chain tying her to me now.

I'll never love another woman—the bond assures that. It also ensures that as long as she hates me, I'll never be happy. Because that's what a soldier is.

A guardian, a lover, a husband. Not that she'll ever accept me now.

Hell, it's been fifty years since we were even in the same room together. But that's my fault. After I saved her ass from assassins, I got the bright idea to kiss her, and she almost took my fucking head off. Likely didn't because she'd lose hers, too.

The memory of her body in my arms and her lips on mine filters through my brain. The way her eyes glowed white, the way her mouth parted. Then it all came crashing down when she punched me hard enough to bloody her own lip.

"What the fuck?" I growled, reaching for her again. I'd wanted to wipe the blood away, but my kindness just made her angrier.

"Thanks for the assist, but you and I both know you only saved me to save yourself."

Fates, the hate on her face made me want to scream. "You. I saved you, because... You know what? Never mind. It doesn't matter what I say, you'll always believe the worst in me."

Her face twisted for just a moment, an ounce of regret

there before her expression hardened once more. "You're right. I will. You killed—"

"I know what I did. And I've paid for it—relived it—every fucking day for a century." In an effort not to touch her, I raked a hand through my hair, careful not to rip it from the roots. "But I can't change the past. What I've done...or how—"

"Don't finish that sentence, Rhys. Don't you fucking dare. We're bonded, yes, but that's it."

That was the last time we spoke—the last time I felt her eyes on me. The last time I felt a glimmer of hope that she might change her mind.

As long as she hates me, I'll never be what I'm meant to be.

But at least I can keep her safe.

Scratching my scruff, I use the rearview mirror to keep an eye on the side door to the gallery. It's an awkward angle, the collar of my shirt digging into my skin as I crane my neck.

Fucking tie.

Loosening the knot, I curse at myself. I don't know why I bothered to put the damn thing on. I never go into the building. Every single time I come to her openings, I hide in the car and watch the door like a damn coward.

Usually, I borrow a car from a friend, but tonight, I'm stuck in my rusted-out shit-box of a truck with no

AC in a bullshit suit that she'll never see. I really should trade up, but this old girl's been with me for twenty years. Letting women go has never been my strong suit.

Finally, I sack up and get out of the cab. The slamming of the door results in a nice little rust confetti shower on the gutter and a loud grating shriek of metal.

So much for subterfuge.

I figure if I keep to the shadows, I can prevent Aurelia from freaking out and keep my ass out of hot water. I'd rather not get stabbed, or shot, or worse— fried. The fried thing hurts like a bitch. But I suppose she has a good reason to be sore at me.

I killed her husband. And allowed our bond without her consent. But how was I to know what would happen? How was I to know that in tying us together, she would lose everything?

It never mattered to her that I didn't choose any of this. I killed him. In a way, I even took her child from her. I did it to save her—to keep her from a fate worse than death.

But some part of me—a big part—is glad he's dead. What kind of monster does that make me, huh? Since the day I learned of their marriage, I wanted what he had—wanted the life he'd found for himself. Wanted her.

I killed my best friend to save her life.

And I've been trying to make up for it ever since.

Crossing the street, I make my way to the side entrance. Like always, the door will be propped open, Evan and her ever-present romantic streak constantly offering an in with Aurelia. She knows I'll be close by, and eventually, I'll man up and get my ass in there.

Just as I creak the door open, several gunshots ring out.

What. The. Fuck.

Ducking my head, a century's worth of training kicks in and I move in a low crouch through the hall toward the main gallery. Said gallery that incidentally contains the source of the gunfire. Pausing for a second, I assess my situation, touching each weapon as if they were my own personal worry stones.

Smith & Wesson M&P40 in my right hip holster, backup mags at my left. Ruger SR40c in the left shoulder holster, extra mags in my right. Backup gun in the shoulder holster, thin Morganite blade at my right ankle lead-lined knife sheath. Small .38 Special five-shot at my left ankle.

While I'm loaded for bear, I could probably be covered in every single weapon I own and not be prepared for what I'm about to see. Peeking past an industrial-looking I-beam, I survey the wreckage of Aurelia's show. The food table has been knocked over, appetizers strewn everywhere. The detritus of cloth napkins and China plates scatter over the concrete floor. Paintings litter the ground or hang haphazardly on the walls, their frames cracked, their canvases gouged with bullets. The crowd is gone, save for a few wounded patrons.

Evan is missing from the melee, but being what she is, it's probably a good thing.

No one wants Evan to lose it. Including me.

I know Aurelia is alive, and she's here, and since I'm not bleeding anywhere, I know she isn't, either. It's one of the few benefits of our screwed-up bond: I'll always know when she's bleeding or injured.

Still, I don't see her.

What I do see is the thickly tattooed arm of an oracle's soldier, and as I peer farther around my cover, I notice he doesn't look so good. He's wearing a bullet-proof vest, yes, but it appears shredded from the number of rounds pumped into it. He's covered in blood from what looks like a double-tap headshot, a thick graze to the jugular, and to top it off, the poor bastard has a pair of wicked-looking throwing knives where his eyes should be.

A phoenix can receive a wound that will "kill" us for a few days, but we will regenerate and get back up once we've healed, unless we're injured with Morganite. So wounds that are considered mortal to humans are still mortal wounds, because while we're healing, we are completely inert.

No breathing. No heartbeat. As dead as dead can be.

For a little while, anyway.

I made a medical examiner nearly shit himself when I popped up on a morgue slab after I'd been declared dead two days prior. That took some explaining. Sometimes humans are a nuisance. Though, given the fact that the man provided a pair of scrubs and a turkey sandwich after he got over his shock, it is possible that humans might not be so bad.

With the healing required for the trio of mortal wounds, it will be a long while before he is up again.

His buddy is still standing, though, and in full tactical gear, save the Kevlar helmet. Since he's also a soldier, he seems to have lost his shirt so he can be a douchebag and display his Legion markings. Like the rest of us, they cover his entire right arm, his right pectoral, and right scapula.

He's wounded, too, with a few metal slivers as thin as knitting needles impaled in his left shoulder, thigh, and shin. He has Aurelia pinned down behind another I-beam, peppering gunfire with an awful *ping-ping-ping* against the metal. But my girl? She's far too crafty for him, and he has run out of bullets faster than expected. I raise my weapon, ready to sever the poor bastard's spinal cord.

Before I have a chance to pull the trigger, Aurelia has abandoned her sanctuary of steel and has launched herself at him. Wearing a pair of black slacks that cup her tight ass like the hand of God, she flies from the I-beam, her ink-covered arms pumping as she sprints toward him.

Fury is stamped all over her face as her raven hair streams behind her, her eyes glowing white even behind those stupid contacts she has to wear to blend in. She has the hilt of one throwing knife in her left hand, and her right hand is empty, her fingers pulled into a tight fist.

Three bounds cross the ten yards that separated them and then she's on him, leaping to hook her legs around his shoulders and hauling his carcass to the ground in an MMA maneuver I've forgotten the name of. His guns are history, having skid across the room in the takedown, and Aurelia has him pinned with a knife to his throat. Her right hand is now grasping his jaw, her fingers digging into his flesh.

Knowing she's most likely going to use the electricity that courses under her skin to fry the fuck out of this dude, I scan my surroundings to see if I'm standing on something conductive. While most of the flooring is concrete, steel beams stand like sentries through the whole building like lightning rods. Yeah... *electricity bad,* especially since if I burn, so does she. I need to stop her before she disintegrates this asshole.

Questioning him might be beneficial.

"Aurelia, *stop,*" I shout, but she's not listening.

Of course she's not. When has she ever listened to me?

Never. The answer is never.

As quick as I can, I rush her, hooking my arm around her waist, keeping her from lighting this entire building up like Christmas morning. Flipping her over, I try to keep her hands away from me while also trying to keep from knocking her around. I'm only marginally success-ful, and now we have matching cuts on our left cheek.

I'm lucky she didn't take my eye out. But we've got bigger problems than some piddly little nick. The soldier has reached his guns, albeit he's hobbling like an old man. It's completely possible she damaged his spine in that MMA move. Only he seems to be having trouble concentrating because he's still trying to chamber a round.

Seriously? Did Iva send the bottom of the barrel, or what?

"Time to go," I say as I try to scoop her compact little body up, but she's having none of it.

"Don't *touch* me, you *abominable* prick," she screams at the same time she realizes it's me, slapping my hands from her waist.

Normally, she'd try to kill me. Again. But I think the soldier is a bigger threat than I am at this point.

"I was trying to keep you from frying me. Don't blame me for attempting to save your life. Again," I growl, irritated I can't even be the good Samaritan with this woman.

"I wasn't in danger of losing my life, you moron. I am perfectly aware of where I am and the simple fact I'm basically in a metal box. I'm also aware of how the laws of conductivity work, as well as a vast number of other laws of fucking physics. I'm not trying to kill anyone else, and there are some wounded people still here. I was just going to slit his throat like a good little girl."

Well, that takes the righteous wind right out of my sails.

"Oh. Well. Sorry?" I shrug just as the soldier finally heals enough to figure out how to work the firearm in his hand.

"You plan on killing this guy, or are you waiting for him to blow my head off with that hand cannon?" she asks, raising her eyebrows at me.

I lift my weapon and fire two rounds into the

soldier's shoulder. Glancing back at her, I quip, "I'd planned on questioning him first."

"Oh." She frowns. "That's smart."

"You can be smart on the physics. I'll be smart on the tactics, Gorgeous," I tease, using the nickname I know she hates.

She rolls her eyes at me and flips me off over her shoulder as she strides over to the soldier, hauling his huge body up off the floor with one hand to the collar of his vest like a pissed-off mama cat. She shakes him viciously, the entire two-hundred-plus pounds of him flopping with the movement.

"Want to tell me why you're shooting up my friend's gallery? Or shall I kill you now, hmm?"

His mouth tightens into a grimace, his heavy brow pulling into a frown.

"I don't think he's going to talk to you," I quip, a hard-won expression of earnestness on my face.

Aurelia's gaze moves from the poor bastard dangling from her grip to me, and I wish I hadn't said anything at all.

"Oh, he'll talk to me. Or I'll take out the Morganite knife stuck in your right boot and carve him like a fucking pumpkin."

Skippy pales at the glow of Aurelia's eyes and the slightly sadistic quality to the curve of her lips. He should be worried. Very worried. She drops him to the concrete with a mighty thud.

"How'd you know I had a knife in my right boot?"

She points to her chest and says, "Seer. Duh."

"So you knew I was here?"

"Of course I did. I know every time you're here, what weapons you carry, and even what color your socks are. Navy and black do not match, BTW. It's the important stuff I can't see. Like who sent this dipshit, but I bet I can guess. Let me see," she says as she reaches for his left shoulder to twist the spike, inciting a pained howl. "Wanna tell me your name?"

"Thad," he gasps. "My name is Thad."

"And who sent you, Thad?" she asks sweetly, which is all the more frightening, given the malevolent expression on her face.

To tell you the truth, I'm feeling a little excluded from this interrogation, so when Thad refuses to answer her, I rip out the spike still protruding from his thigh with a vicious jerk. The agonized scream turns my stomach a little, but it does the job because now Thad can't stop talking.

"Iva. Iva sent me," he gasps. "She sent me to stall you because she has more soldiers coming. She's going to capture you this time, and it doesn't matter what he"—He nods at me—"does to save you. He has a price on his head, too." Thad's breathing hard, panting as if his lungs have decided this very minute is the time to work double-time.

Iva. That slippery little bitch. I've been dodging our Primary—our leader—for over a hundred and fifty years. Just her name sends a shudder down my spine.

Aurelia reaches into my shoulder holster and pulls out the Ruger. She chambers a round and pumps it into his head with enough quickness I don't have the chance to stop her.

I'd yell at her, given that we still needed more info, but the expression of pure, unadulterated terror on Aurelia's face is enough to make me shut up and move.

"We have to go. Now," I say as I take the Ruger from her and re-holster it.

Grabbing her ice-cold hand in mine, I head for the back of the gallery toward the rear parking lot while asking, "Where's Evan?"

"She was losing it, so I made her go ahead of me to ready the cabin. She's safe."

A sigh of relief has my shoulders drooping just a little. "Thank you for keeping her safe."

She swallows thickly. "She's a better sister than I ever got. I'd do anything to make sure that little shit stays breathing."

Aurelia's family shit is the stuff of legend. I've never

seen a mother as uptight or unrelenting as hers. Nothing was ever good enough. Aurelia wasn't polite enough, proper enough. It didn't help that she didn't want the role she was born into. It didn't matter to her family what kind of daughter they had—they'd rather have her twin. A sister—as time went on—who shunned her just as harshly as her parents did.

We reach the door, and she pulls me toward a slate-gray, new model Dodge Challenger SRT Hellcat. She drops my hand suddenly as if she'd forgotten she hates me for those few minutes and has just remembered. To ease the newly forming ache in my chest, I take a split second to admire the awesomeness of the vehicle before me, holding my hand out for the keys.

She gives me a look of indignation before reaching under the front driver's side wheel well for her spare key. She shakes her head, presses the key fob, and opens the door to slide in behind the wheel.

"Nobody drives my baby but me."

Throwing my hands up in surrender, I slip into the passenger seat. "Can't blame a guy for trying."

She shrugs as if to give me the point while pushing the ignition button. Peeling out of the lot, she weaves into traffic with an ease I've never seen any driver pull off—driving better than even I can, which is irritating to say the very least.

I'd never tell her, though—she'd have to torture it out of me first.

The wail of sirens start just as we reach the third block out, and four squad cars followed by a SWAT bus scream past us in a blur of speed. It's not like in the movies. No one looks at us. No one suspects we had anything to do with the carnage those poor fellows will walk into.

From what I can feel and see, I know she is uninjured, but I need to know she is all right, though.

"We're going to be fine, you know that, right?" I say, trying to reassure her.

Her face is a blank mask, her thoughts and emotions expertly hidden from me. Her only tell is the grayish-white cast to her knuckles as they grip the wheel.

"I know we will. It's the next part that worries me."

"What's that?" I ask, on edge because knowing Aurelia, it could be anything.

"We have to be in the same car. Together. And driver picks the music," she quips with an evil smile.

Fates, please not—

Of course. Taylor Swift comes out of the speakers just to torture me. Aurelia shimmies in her seat as she punches the beautiful beast into fifth gear.

"You're the Devil," I grouse, crossing my arms, doing my damnedest not to stare at her boobs as she laughs in her seat. The brief glimpse of joy on her face is everything to me, though.

"Well, I can't kill you or inflict any wounds without hurting myself, so Tay-Tay is what you get. Suck it up, buttercup." She smiles as she pops the "P" with her lips.

I feel like she's probably going to torture me forever. I hate that she hates me—that she can't see my side of things.

"You could have just left me there, you know," I murmur, the sting of her rejection twisting the knife in my chest.

"I know I could have. But if they caught you, they'd kill you to kill me. It's a no-brainer, really. I'm helping you to save my own ass. And as soon as I figure out how to remove our binding, I'll never see your face again. Sound like a plan?"

She glances my way, but I school my features long enough to nod. That little quip twists the knife again, and I have to grit my teeth against the ache. Removing the binding, even as hard as it is to bear, would be like cutting off a limb—like cutting out my heart.

"Sounds like you've got it all worked out," I croak, staring out the window at the passing traffic, as we head north on I-25 out of town.

I know this for certain: I am going to get this girl to forgive me if it's the last thing I do.

4

AURELIA

AFTER FIVE AND A HALF HOURS OF DRIVING, ONE FUEL STOP, and a circuitous route, we've made it to the safe house in Grand Lake, or the "cabin mountain on steroids" as Evan calls it. The safe house is more her father's vacation cabin than anything else. I've only seen pictures of it, but they didn't do it justice.

The exterior can only be described as a log cabin's hotter, older, manlier brother. Thick logs run the perimeter of the four-story house, only broken up by large picture windows lit up in the gloom of the night sky. Craggy stone columns bookend the porch, solidly constructed of immense limestone slabs and broad vertical logs. The very top floor seems much smaller than the ones below, possibly serving as a loft or crow's nest for surveillance.

Security doesn't appear to be a concern here. The house is alone on the top of a large foothill surrounded on three sides by the Rocky Mountain National Park, with the closest neighbor half a mile out in any direction. The hundred-acre property is solidly enclosed by a rough stone wall tall enough to classify the place as a fortress.

Getting through the gate is easier than I expected, especially since the security panel at the eight-foot, iron entry gate requires my thumbprint. I'm going to have to talk to Evan about her lack-of-privacy shtick.

My thumbprint? Really?

Several cars and trucks dot the cabin's half-mile driveway: a shiny Jaguar interspersed with late model Fords, and a new Audi mixed with a rusted-out Chevy. I park in the only open spot, incidentally only twenty feet from the front door, and roughly punch the button to turn off the ignition after shifting my baby into park.

Man, I miss the days when you could turn a key. Simply pressing a button just doesn't have the same air of purpose.

Groaning, I open the car door and pull my body to standing. I rub my eyes, so happy I ditched the contacts and shake out my legs before going to the trunk to pull out my go-bag. Every vehicle I own has a small duffel bag stashed somewhere inside them. They contain cash, clothes, one day of rations (*beef jerky and a flask of Jameson—don't give me too much credit*), and a shiny new identity.

The identity I probably won't need just yet, but I will need the set of clothes—my suit jacket lost to poor George, my pants and shirt ruined by Thad's inter-rogation.

I feel guilty for not using the Morganite knife and killing him for real since I know he'll heal in the next couple of days. My only solace is that it will take a few days to regrow his whole fucking head. *Dick.*

I knew I shouldn't have gone to that stupid exhibit. I swear it's the last time I let Evan talk me into anything.

And I mean it this time.

Rhys was quiet most of the drive, a blessing because I had no idea what to say to him. But it's a curse, too, the barbed guilt of my silence running through my veins. I've spent little time with him that hasn't included me trying to rip him limb from limb, so a conversation might've been impossible. Plus, I'm a little disturbed that having him so close for so long hasn't been the hardship I always thought it would be.

He was quiet, considerate, and he pumped the gas when we stopped, because me getting out of the car would have probably gotten the police called on us. He even got me snacks when he went in to pay.

It's tough to be bitchy to a man that brings me foodstuffs.

And for every minute of those five and a half hours, I had to fight the two warring sides of my brain. One side completely ruled by hate and fear, telling me it's all his fault, even though I know it isn't. The other side worries if he's taking care of himself and likes that he came to help—even if I didn't really need it.

Both sides need to shut the hell up.

Rhys and I meet at the back of the car. He reaches past me to lift my duffel out of the trunk, not even letting me carry my own luggage—the bastard. He raises his eyebrows, almost asking permission, and I nearly lose it. If he'd cooperate and be an asshole so I could hate him appropriately, that'd be great.

Grinding my teeth together in an attempt to avoid screaming, I give him a jerky nod and let him take the bag. It requires a bit of effort, but I gently close my trunk, careful not to hurt my baby—even though I want to smash something.

I stride toward the front door behind Rhys, vigilantly trying not to stomp my feet and pout like a toddler. My anger only grows when I notice how spectacular he looks in a suit.

Holy shit balls.

Being away from him so long, I always forget the pull he has on me. Easily six foot three—maybe taller— he towers over me like a fucking monolith. I'm five-three on a good day, so he's at least an entire foot taller than me. The crisp charcoal-gray suit caresses the wideness of his shoulders and the line of his body as it flows from his strong neck to his lean waist and tight ass.

People I hate are not supposed to be this hot in a suit.

He's not hot. It's just the bond, remember? It's bullshit magic clouding your head. You hate him.

I'm pretty sure being pissed at Rhys is all that's holding me together at this point. Flashes of the wounded humans, blood leaking through fingers, gasps of final breaths bombard my brain, and I swallow hard. Screwing my eyes shut, I try to blot out the horror on their faces of the people as they ran past me. The sight of the young woman who fell close to the back entrance and got stomped on by fifteen people before someone was brave enough to haul her up. The expression of unadulterated fear on Evan's face when I slapped the shit out of her, snapping her out of her shock.

Before Rhys can reach the porch, Evan bursts out of the front door like a jack-in-the-box, followed at a more sedate pace by an incredibly large man who seems capable of murder. Evan's long curly blonde hair flies behind her as she sprints toward me, her wide blue eyes set with determination, a frown pulling at her elfin face. She runs right past Rhys, plowing her shoulder into his gut with enough force, he nearly biffs it on the asphalt driveway. He's saved at the last second by the burly dude, who could give Paul Bunyan a run for his money in the height department.

Instead of the fear I expect, she practically climbs me like a tree and attack-hugs me with enough strength to bruise my ribs and squeezes the breath from my lungs. I never knew the little blonde pixie had it in her. And I do mean pixie. If Evan says she's over five feet, she's lying her ass off.

"I'm so sorry, Ari. Please forgive me," she whisper-sobs in my ear, fully latching onto me like a baby koala.

"For what, baby doll?" I murmur, gently rubbing her back, trying to calm her down. "You didn't do anything wrong."

As horrible as I feel for slapping her, Evan can turn into your worst nightmare if she gets pissed off. The power running under her skin rivals even her father's, and she's a baby. Usually, only the old ones have the kind of juice that she has to keep bottled up, and she's barely over a century old. It's supposed to take *several* centuries to hone those types of powers, and she's had to harness them in her little body for barely more than one.

"I—I did. I was scared of you, and you didn't deserve it. You snapped me back when I could have done something stupid, or fully lost it and hurt someone. Fates, I'm such a *freak*."

"Evangeline Marie Black," I growl, full-naming her just like her mother would. "You are not a freak, you little shit, so stop talking like that. You are special in the best way possible. If I hear you talk bad about yourself again, I'll singe all your hair off, so help me."

My quip shakes a laugh from deep in her belly, and she climbs down to the asphalt, returning quickly for a squeeze before wiping her eyes and nose.

"Calm down, I got it. No need to murder my beautiful hair. That would be a crime against nature, or against the Geneva Convention, or something." She gestures to her perfectly tousled blonde ringlets.

"Oh," she says, bouncing right into the next subject, "I meant to tell you, I popped back to the gallery after letting Dad know the skinny of what was going on. I took care of the security cameras in the gallery as well as the surrounding buildings. I don't know if there are backups to the digital footage or not, but the originals should be gone. Also, I made sure no identifying info is at the gallery, and since you go through a shell company for your royalties, I don't think anyone can trace you through there."

Evan has a proficiency for covering shit up. As she should. Puberty rage, plus a girl who can decimate an entire town in minutes? Girlfriend has experience. Her teen years were hell on wheels to say the least. Just don't look too far into the history of the 1906 earthquake in San Francisco.

So *not* an earthquake.

That's where I met Evan. In the middle of all that fire and ruin, half out of her mind with rage and about to burn to death. I had to knock the shit out of her then, too.

"What about you? Shouldn't you be there now? Aren't the cops still there?"

I'm stunned she got so much accomplished so fast.

"I gave my statement hours ago," she answers with a nonchalant wave of her hand. "You took an age getting here. Did you get lost or something? It's on the news already."

"Not all of us can whisper around like freaking smoke, nerd. Some of us have to drive. Some of us have to make sure we weren't followed. Did any of the wounded make it?"

She nods somberly. "The dude with the gut shot died in surgery, but I'm not at all surprised. I'm amazed he lived as long as he did. The chick with the arm graze is stable, no arterial damage, but I think the docs are going to repair the nerve damage after the initial swelling goes down. The guy that passed out near the exit is going to be fine—he just has a concussion. The other two ladies died from blood loss—they were dead before they hit the floor."

I incline my head, agonized at the massacre one little show caused. I can't believe after all these years, after all the life I've sacrificed, I'm here running from that bitch again. One fucking art show. Shame climbs up my throat for every single human that was hurt or killed—the burn of guilty tears stinging my eyes and nose. I feel the heat of a body sliding close to me.

"Can we get inside now that you're done with your little debriefing?" Rhys asks as he grabs my hand and drags me into the house. "I don't want Ari out here, even if it is in the middle of nowhere."

For a second, safety and warmth grip me. Then I remember why holding his hand is a bad thing. I shake off his fingers as if his flames would actually burn me. "I don't like being touched, douchebag. Especially by you."

Heat creeps up my cheeks at the scene I'm making, and I nearly shake my head. I'm blushing like some stupid virgin girl in a historical romance novel *at the mere touch of the duke's hand.* For fuck's sake, I think I hate myself.

Rhys looks back at me with an unreadable expression that slowly morphs into a little upturn of his lips. Now I'm looking at his lips. *Son of a bitch.* Can I be any more transparent?

I have *got* to get out of here.

Directing my attention to Evan and her brute of a companion, I examine him closely, taking in his wide stance, thick thighs, and sturdy motorcycle boots. His dark hair is pulled from his face into a man-bun, making his jade-green eyes pop. He would be considered beautiful, or at least I assume so, if I could see what lay beneath the mountain of a beard taking up residence on his face. His appearance screams "tough guy," with the copious tattoos on his forearms and thick gauges in his ears, or at least it would if I weren't covered in ink myself.

He has a hand on Evan's shoulder as he steers her into the house. Then it dawns on me. This is the guardian that has been lurking in the shadows for the last several decades—since the '20s, I think. Evan has never introduced him to me, but I've always known he was there, looking out for her, making sure she was safe. Where the hell he was today is anyone's guess.

Facing him, I ask, "What's your name?"

I know it already, but hearing him speak will tell me so much more.

"West," he grunts at me, crossing his arms in such a way it discourages further questions.

"Do you have a last name, West?" I ask, arching a perturbed brow. "What do you do here? And more importantly, where the fuck were you today? 'Cause, I gotta say, your absence when she could have gotten killed is not sitting so well with me."

"Don't worry, Ari," Evan assures me. "It's not his fault. He's simply doing what he's told, aren't you, West?" She says this in such an ominous manner, I'm a little scared for the poor guy.

Glancing past the menacing little wraith, I take in the interior of the safe house. An enormous stone fireplace dominates the great room, the open floor plan leaving the kitchen and a library nook in plain view. The walls are log planked, the décor decidedly rustic with chandeliers made from antlers, and buttery tan leather furniture adorned with plaid throw pillows.

There are two winding staircases on each side of the large opening to the kitchen. One staircase—that appears to be constructed solely of pine logs and branches—leads to the upper floors, and the other seems to lead down to the bottom level. Each of the rooms have large, unadorned picture windows looking out to the view below. The night is dark as pitch, but the moonlight reflects like a mirror on the lake at the base of the mountain.

Evan wraps an arm around my waist and steers me down the hall toward the stairs to the bottom level. Coming from the bottom of the staircase is the sound of male laughter and what I'm assuming is a game room if the sound of clacking billiards is any indication.

"Let's go see Dad before we get you settled."

"Aww! Do I have to? Your dad hates me," I complain, dragging my feet, but the little powerhouse pulls me along as if I weigh nothing.

"He doesn't hate you. He's just angry you won the last round of sparring." She shoots me a censuring look over her shoulder. "Did you have to beat him so badly? He practically had to turn in his man card on that one."

A sly smile slides across my face. Yes, I needed to kick his sorry ass for thinking a *poor, weak woman* couldn't knock his ass into next Tuesday. He should have known better.

I hear two deep chuckles behind me and realize I said the last bit aloud.

Oops.

Glancing back, West—whose face seems to be made of granite and frowns—has cracked a smile. I guess old John isn't everyone's favorite person.

Evan's father, John Black, is a hard man, but for better or worse, I respect him. I'd be stupid not to. And while his motives and mind games might be centuries in the making, he loves and protects my best friend.

"He's the one who said no powers." I shrug. "It's not my fault I train every day."

What I don't say—because it can get me killed—is that I didn't go full blast. I didn't even break a sweat, handing the Wraith King his ass without a smidgen of effort. I figure he either rigged it so I would win—the purpose for which I'm not sure—or he's letting me know he's weak.

Either way, I'm positive I'm not going to like the answer.

5

RHYS

We reach the entrance of what is, in fact, a game room, and the conversation grinds to an immediate halt. One, lone, billiard ball, plunking into its rightful pocket is the last sound to be heard. As I hit the bottom stair behind the girls, I feel the frisson of a threat in the room, the hair on my arms standing on end.

Aurelia might have her visions, but I have a fully developed sense of when shit is about to hit the fan. Before she can move, I drop the duffel and step in front of her. With my body, I block whatever attack may come, my arm reaching back to clutch her to me. If we need to escape, she's coming with me—I don't care if I have to throw her over my shoulder like a fucking caveman.

I've done it before, and I'll do it again.

I manage to refrain from drawing a weapon—not that it would do any good—but it is a near thing. In the presence of a king, drawing a weapon would be a one-way ticket to a death I wouldn't be able to regenerate from.

"Well, well, if it isn't the runaway oracle and her boy toy," a deep voice rumbles, rough as gravel but with a spark of humor.

The man attached to it isn't tall nor is he short. John Black's features are nondescript: medium-brown hair threaded through with silver, medium-brown eyes, slim straight nose, thick straight eyebrows.

Even his name is unremarkable.

To the eye, he's nothing special. But looks can be deceiving.

His daughter and her guardian have been my friends for many, many years, but I have yet to meet John. And while the king still owes me a boon, meeting him hasn't been high up on my to-do list. It may have something to do with the battles I fought against the wraiths when I was still a member of my Legion, still under the thumb of our Primary, Iva. Or it could be that my family—my brother in particular—was tasked with killing John's wife.

Dealer's choice.

My brother failed in his endeavor, and I made sure Olivia Black survived the attack on her home. I sold out my own brother to the enemy because I didn't like the sanctioned murder of an innocent woman. Killing is not a phoenix's purpose. So, I put a stop to it.

Delivering my brother to the wraiths seemed like my only option at the time. Phoenixes are supposed to be good. We're supposed to send souls on to be reborn.

Not change the future.

Not kill the innocent.

Nothing but helping souls move on.

Iva's been changing the game for centuries, twisting it, and us as a species, into something ugly. I threw a wrench in the spokes of her evil wheel by letting Olivia Black live, and in turn, Evan was born.

"John." I offer him an abbreviated nod in deference instead of the full bow expected of me, my arm still clutching Aurelia to my back, keeping her out of the way.

No way in hell am I taking my eyes off him, or the seven men scattered throughout the room like land mines, no matter what Evan said about proper protocol.

Each man has the appearance of leisure, lounging on couches, leaning against the pool table, sitting on bar stools with beer bottles in their hands, but I know differently. One, or maybe none of these men are my friends.

Safe house my ass.

Just as I think the dam of tension will break and kill us all, John calmly rises from his stool. Striding over to me, he takes my hand in his firm grip and slaps my shoulder in greeting. His mouth—that had been set in a hard line—turns up into a smile, and each of the seven men in the room relaxes their posture to one of true leisure.

But what's more disconcerting is the gusting breath of relief that wheezes from West's lips. When I was counting threats—like an idiot—I hadn't counted him. While he's been my friend for the better part of a century, I'm not altogether sure which way West would lean if it came to blows between the king and me.

"I'm glad you got out safely," he says with a warm smile, nodding to Aurelia. "Though, I'm not sure it was a question you would with both of you there."

She moves from my grasp, cautiously positioning herself a step behind me. I look back at Aurelia and see her face is carefully blank, her wide full lips slightly parted on an indrawn breath. Her shoulders are relaxed and loose, but after years of observing her, I can tell it's more in preparation to strike rather than a gesture of good will. Her eyes flick from John's to mine, and in the nearly mint-green gaze is a hint of unease.

I know I'm right to be wary right now. Keeping my body relaxed, my mind tenses, my spine burns, and my wings ache to break free.

"All it takes is one lucky shot," she says. "Even I know that."

I think she's referring more to her win over John than Thad's quick demise, deferring to the king.

"Well, either way, it's good you got out of there. From what Evan and West told me, soon after you left, the place was swarming with soldiers. After you've cleaned up, I think we need to have a discussion about how safe you guys are here. Please, make yourselves comfortable and we'll meet back down here when you are ready."

Bowing my head, I realize we're being dismissed. She may hate it, but I take Aurelia's hand, tugging her behind me as we wind our way back up the circular staircase.

The real problem comes when we get to the door to our room. Evan, being the consummate matchmaker, hopeless romantic, and all-around pain in my ass, has decided Aurelia and I are rooming together.

She gestures between the two of us, then to the door we've stopped in front of. "This is you."

While I have zero problems sharing a room with Aurelia, I cringe in preparation of the shouting I'm almost positive is coming.

"You're fucking with me, right?" Aurelia asks in a low voice.

I'm not sure she realizes she's still holding my hand or not, but if she hasn't, I'm not going to be the one to tell her.

"There are only seven rooms in this house, even with the Murphy beds in the office and the pull-out in the game room. There are thirteen people here. I know the house is big, but where in the hell do you think they're all going to sleep? Plus, Dad has a rule about guardians and their charges sleeping in the same room. I'm even bunking with West." Evan shrugs, barely glancing down at our entwined fingers.

"Speaking of the plethora of men—what the fuck are all these people doing here?" Aurelia hisses. "When I said ready the cabin, I did not mean call every warrior and their brother to come guard us. I meant turn the lights and the hot tub on and get some booze. What's going on?" Aurelia's so mad she's almost stammering.

"I'm going to have to tell you about it later. I don't know if you realize this, but you're still covered in blood.

Go take a shower, please. When you're done, come find me. I'll be in the loft," Evan quips and flounces away as if Aurelia wouldn't tackle her where she stands.

It takes everything I have not to bust up laughing right there in the hall. Aurelia's head whips to me as she burns me with a glare, releasing my hand to push her way into the room.

And that's when Aurelia sees red. An enormous four-poster bed dominates the room—its ornate posts and top covered in gauzy white fabric. The heavy, baroque side tables hold vases of flowers and glass-bowled lamps. Across from the bed is a stone-faced fire-place with a fire already burning in the grate. Even in July, the mountains are cold in Colorado, especially in the evenings.

What's worse, the lights have been dimmed, and there are candles burning on almost every available surface. It's like the honeymoon suite of a Harlequin romance novel threw up in here. And I'm obviously not the only one who thinks this if Aurelia's low, menacing growl is any indication.

"Are you kidding me?" she grits, her hands curled into fists.

She seems to be working exceptionally hard not to throw sparks or flame up and burn this whole house down. After the day she's had, I have to commend her on the effort. Or I would if the thing she's so pissed about is being in a room with me.

Tossing my hands up in surrender, I heave a sigh. "Don't blame me. I didn't do the room assignments."

"Whatever," she huffs. "She's right: I do need a shower." Aurelia snatches the duffle from my fingers, slamming the attached bathroom door as she goes.

That could have gone worse.

RHYS—1855

I should have said something before now, I thought as I observed Aurelia's rising blush, but it never crossed my mind Lucien would betray me this way.

Aurelia was a tiny slip of a woman—barely over five feet—but her personality made her so much taller than any meager inch she may have possessed. Her golden skin—so much darker than the pale humans in the next town—was still stained a delicate, glowing pink. In all the years I'd known her, I'd never seen her blush, and the thought of Lucien inciting such a reaction from her set my teeth on edge.

In my head, she had always been mine. I knew it was stupid to think that way—about a woman who hadn't paid me even a lick of attention—but I'd loved her for so long.

She'd been promised to me—the bastard knew it, and still...

Lucien and I used to be friends—closer than brothers—almost inseparable.

Before Selection, we were practically family. After Selection, I lost my best friend. It wasn't as if I'd gotten a choice of placement. Lucian had known we could play soldier and dream all we wanted, but in the end, the Primary chose our fate.

Lucien was selected to be a scholar—an honorable profession in our society. But me? I was chosen to be what Lucien had always wanted to be—a soldier. Aurelia's soldier to be exact, and in that decision, one day I would get what I wanted more than anything on this earth—to be Aurelia's husband.

Not that she knew it.

She wouldn't accept me—that, I knew for certain. In her mind, whomever the Primary chose for her wouldn't be an option. Ever.

She would never bind herself to me—not of her free will.

Aurelia was not the type of woman who liked to be told what to do, and in a matriarchal society such as ours, usually that wasn't a bad thing. But Aurelia hated the life she'd been borne into. Hated what she was destined for. Hated her eyes, which had dictated the course of her life from the first day they fluttered open.

Those pale, pupilless orbs cemented her destiny as an oracle—and her hatred for me.

Lucien had known how much I burned for her. From the very first day I heard her argue with her mother, I was lost.

"I would rather eat a pinecone than wear that silly corset, Mother. There is absolutely no reason to adhere to a societal norm of a society in which I have no interest in participating."

She was ten, and I twelve, and I knew then that I would do anything for her. But that was before I was a soldier. Before Julian lost his mind and his sense of right and wrong. Before I seriously debated committing treason.

Now, my love would come at a price—a price I never wanted her to pay. If I did what I'd set out to do, Aurelia would be in danger.

Lucien crowded her, putting himself in her space much closer than polite society would allow, but Aurelia didn't appear to mind one bit. She gazed up at him, grinning, happy—until she felt my eyes on her. She shifted her gaze to me, her blush paling as her smile fell. An expression of fear passed over her features, and she dropped her head to stare at the vegetables she was purchasing. She thought I'd tell or cause a scene.

Oh, how wrong she was.

To fight the urge to rip his head off, I pivoted from the woman I coveted more than anything on this planet, attempting to school my features into something resembling calm.

I didn't hate Lucien. I envied him. Because he had her love. He had her trust. He had her, and while I could possibly one day have her future, I wouldn't be her first love. I wouldn't be her first anything—except maybe her first hate.

"Rhys, I need to talk to you," a voice called from behind me—Lucien's voice.

Of course he needs to talk to me.

I halted my quick clip through the forest on my way to the cliff top—needing to fly, to be free, if only for a little while. So naturally, I would get stopped when I was a meager inch away from losing my mind.

"What do you need, Lucien?" I growled, not turning around. I didn't want to see his smug, gloating smile—otherwise I'd likely punch it right off his stupid face.

"I have a problem. I'm pretty sure you're the only person I can trust."

"You can't trust me." I chuckled darkly. "You shouldn't even talk to me. I sure as hell don't want to talk to you. Congratulations. You won. She loves you. You'd better love her back, and as long as you do, you don't get to ask a damn thing from me."

I'd made up my mind about a few things. I had to fix my brother, Julian—one way or another—and then I had to leave. Watching them together was the worst sort of Hell.

"How long do you think they are going to wait for her to decide, Rhys? She has pushed and pushed as long as she can, but soon enough, they'll stop asking. They'll decide for her. She's… they… she's carrying my child," he admitted, the words gushed past his lips, slicing their way into my heart.

Lucien's youthful face was lined in worry and fear. Had I ever looked that young? Had I ever been that earnest? Did he honestly believe I wouldn't rip him apart?

"We married in secret months ago. We've kept it from everyone, but she will start to show soon enough." He gripped the back of his neck, his frustration and fear evident. "As soon as we can, we're leaving. But I need help…"

He said more about the Aegis, about Aurelia, about malicious leaders. But I didn't pay much attention to him. The only thing that ran through my head was Lucien's voice telling me I'd never have her.

She's carrying my child. We married in secret.

A strange buzzing took over the thoughts in my head as I left him behind me. My phase ripped through me, the burn of my Fireskin chased away his voice, the ache of my wings bursting from my back providing refuge as I soared off the cliff. The wind whipped through my feathers and past my ears, deadening my senses.

If only for a moment.

6

AURELIA—1855

MOTHER BARRED MY ESCAPE, HER FEATURES LINED IN disapproval, bordering on disgust. She didn't understand me. I wasn't even sure she loved me. In fact, I was almost certain she didn't. In all my life, I had never garnered a smile from her, never a kind word or gentle touch. I couldn't remember the last time I'd been hugged or confided in, or anything resembling the families I'd observed in our community. My family shunned me in private and scolded me in public.

Don't run.

Don't speak so loudly.

Remember your manners.

Act like a lady.

Do what you're told.

After a while, I stopped trying to please them. In their eyes, my sister could do no wrong, so I decided to quit trying to make my family something they were not.

It didn't help that I knew what would happen before it did, or that I knew when humans in the next town— or three towns over for that matter—would pass away. I would always be on the outside.

My eyes made me a pariah in my own home. The seer part of the equation was just icing on the cake.

It was close to suppertime, but it didn't matter for me. I ate my meals separately from them, never within touching distance—but still, she stood, barring my exit. I wondered if I tried to touch her if she'd still stand between me and my freedom. If I yelled and screamed and caused a stir, would she still keep me here?

Perhaps she would, but then again, maybe she wouldn't. I doubted she held me any more than she had to when I was a baby—it was unlikely she'd allow me to come within a foot of her now.

"Where do you think you're going?" she asked as if she had the right. She may have given birth to me, she may have fed me, but she had never given me love.

Not ever.

"I'm leaving this house to see my husband, Mother," I said to her stunned face. I would've admitted I was with child, but honestly, given the puce tinge to her features, she might have combusted where she stood.

"Hu-husband? Have you lost your mind, Aurelia? You have no *right* to take a husband. You are to be an oracle. Your soldier has been chosen for you. You know the rules, *child*. How could you be so careless?"

Oracle. As if I would ever willingly subject myself to the horrors of that job title.

"Careless? The oracle position is not my only option, Mother. I can choose exile, which I would *prefer*, since it is the *only Fates-forsaken* choice I will get to *make*. I would rather make my own fate than take the life someone dictates for me. You should know better. You know I'm not very fond of doing what I'm told, now am I, Mother?"

"You think they will just let you go? Silly little girl." She shook her head, pity clearly written all over her face.

"I spoke to Nicola myself. She said I was allowed to choose as long as I did so before maturity."

"Nicola isn't who I'm worried about," she muttered, and then her eyes widened when she realized what she'd said aloud.

So, it isn't Nicola she is worried about. But if not Nicola...

Iva—our leader, our Primary—was not someone I

ever wished to tangle with. She was the ultimate reason I didn't want to be an oracle in the first place. She frightened me down to my very bones. An ominous sense of dread washed over me every single time I stepped within three feet of her.

It was as if she carried the weight of a thousand souls—as if she were stained in death.

There was no way I would ever be an oracle with her as my leader, and no way I would willingly hand that woman the knife to cut out my eyes. I still couldn't fathom how we had progressed so much as a society and still followed that barbaric practice.

I liked my eyes where they were, thank you very much.

"Did you ever consider that perhaps I see much more than you give me credit for?"

My mother sighed a deep, shuddering breath. "That, my dear, has always been the problem. You see too much," she whispered and stepped out of my way. "If you are set on going, I would go sooner rather than later. Take your young man and leave this place before it is too late."

Her voice, so heavy with foreboding, sent a chill skittering down my spine. It was the kindest she had ever been to me, and I had no idea what to do with her words.

"We are trying to leave before the week is out. Do you think this is enough time?"

"I hope so," was all she said before leaving me alone to decide.

Choosing between my family who had given me life—but not an ounce of love—and a man, who not only gave me the love and affection I so desperately craved, but the child I carried.

It was no contest. I opened the thick, oak door and walked toward my future.

AURELIA

It takes no time at all to get undressed and in the shower. The bathroom is just as lavish as the rest of the house, conveniently stocked for guests. But Evan knows me better than anyone and has all my favorite stuff. Speedily, I wash the blood off my arms and neck with the super-expensive ginger and orange oil body wash. Shampooing my hair twice—because Fates know what's in it—I use a handful of conditioner to tame my wavy locks into submission.

Shutting off the water, I towel off and open my duffle. Inside, I've got five bags of beef jerky—chipotle flavor—my favorite "Fuck My Liver" flask full of Irish whiskey, a quarter-million dollars in varied bills, and a manila envelope containing a whole new identity.

I take the time to braid my hair in a long side tail before dressing in a gray T-shirt, and a pair of jeans with frayed holes in both knees. Sliding on sandals, I clasp my favorite sterling silver feather necklace around my neck and slip a stack of bangles on my wrist.

Throwing open the bathroom door, I find all the candles blown out and an empty room. Lit by a lone bedside lamp, the bedspread is depressed on one side where I assume Rhys had rested for a bit. Despite him giving me the space I demanded, I'm disappointed to not see him here. Irrational anger burns in my gut.

I shouldn't care that he didn't wait for me.

But I do.

I don't care. I hate him.

Yeah, bitch. Keep telling yourself that. How's reality working out for you?

Gritting my teeth, I glance at the bedside clock. I'm bone tired, but I need answers now that I'm done pouting in the bathroom. Even though it's after midnight, I leave our shared room and my bullshit feelings, heading up the stairs to the fourth-floor loft, jingling my bangles the whole way.

I'm doing this because I'm trying to let Evan and

West know I'm coming so they'll stop making out and put some fucking clothes on.

But just like everything else, I know what I'm going to catch them doing, and I'd rather not see it in person. The vivid imagery in my brain is plenty—trust me. I'm pretty sure those two have been dating a while behind everyone's back. How she kept it from me, though, I'm not so sure. It makes me wonder what else she's hiding—the little shit. She's practically been MIA for the last month.

I jingle the bracelets harder, but my warning goes unheeded, and I see way more of my friend's boob than I ever needed to. On the upside, West has a very nice ass, and I can attest he has tattoos just about everywhere. Resting my shoulder on the doorframe, I'm careful to look anywhere but in their direction, shaking my wrist as hard as I can.

Nothing.

"Did the loud-as-shit jingling not tip you off I was coming?" I gripe as they startle apart and hastily begin pulling on clothes.

I scold West's back as he tucks himself into his low-riding jeans. "I could have been anyone in this house, you know. I could have been her dad. Hell, I could have been the enemy. Stop thinking with your dick and pick a room with a door, you moron."

He growls at me through a good-natured smile, but his gaze swiftly goes to my best friend and the look in them says it all.

He loves her. Deeply.

"The loft? Really, Evan? You knew I was coming, jerk, and while you do have a fabulous rack, I don't swing that way and I don't need to see it."

"Sorry." She shrugs. "The time got away from us."

"Evidently," I grumble. "So you two are together? I take it that's not new."

She shakes her head with a sheepish expression, brushing errant curls off her forehead.

"Mazel tov. Maybe sometime you can talk to me about it, you know, when the threat of death isn't so imminent. Sound like a plan?"

Evan lets her smile answer for her.

"So, while I'd love to scrub out my brain with bleach to erase what I've just seen, it's not an option right now. Two questions. Where's Rhys? And what the hell are all these people doing here? Go."

"I think Rhys is in the game room getting to know the guys, and Dad's personal guard is here because there's been some serious unrest going on in our community. I talked to Dad a little bit before you got here, and there have been attacks on wraith families in the surrounding states. Five families are unaccounted for." She pauses, swallowing hard. "Dad thinks the shit is about to hit the fan here, so as soon as he can get some things handled, we're all leaving. He wanted me to extend the invitation to you and Rhys as well."

She's leaving something out. I know she is, but I'll needle her about it later when her Goliath is not in the room.

"Why didn't he say anything earlier?"

"I think it's just Dad being cautious. Never can be too paranoid when it comes to times of war. You know that."

I do. Even your own family can turn on you if you're not too careful.

We make our way down to the game room, the sounds just as raucous as before. Only this time when I arrive, the conversation doesn't halt like a bad '80s movie record scratch. Each of the men continue what they're doing as if I'm not here. I notice Rhys across the room talking to John—his body held in such a way I know interrupting would be a bad idea. Plopping down on a barstool, I survey each of the men.

Across the pool table, sitting on the smaller of the two couches, are two men slightly removed from the rest of the guards. They are arguing in murmured tones in a Portuguese dialect I don't recognize. The one on the left of the couch has smooth, coppery-brown skin, full, almost pouty lips, a head of unruly black hair. He's dressed casually in a plain navy shirt, ripped jeans, and motorcycle boots.

The one on the right has sharper cheekbones and fuller lips, his eyes and hair black as night. His crisp coal-black suit is at odds with the heavy fall of hair across his eyes. He looks pissed as hell, his voice dropping several decibels as his gestures and words turn sharper.

At the pool table in front of me are two men dueling with trash talk. The one at the head of the table is lining up his shot, the tight red shirt stretching across his impressive back. His rich brown skin almost glows in the overhead table light. He laughs at his friend, a white smile stretching across his full lips as his eyes crinkle at the corners.

His friend stands on the other side of the table, his stance wide, leaning on the cue like a crutch. He's extremely tall, a thick wool beanie half-covering his shaggy, dark hair. A week's worth of scruff adorns his face, and his caramel gaze is filled with mischief.

Two disgruntled-looking men sit on the larger couch to my right, their blackened eyes and split lips seem to speak of a story I'm dying to know about. Their postures are rigid, scolded, almost as if they've been sent to the principal's office. The one closest to John appears to be worse off, his Romanesque nose bloody and dripping onto his white T-shirt. His dark hair is in disarray as if he's tried ripping it out recently.

His couch buddy runs a hand over his shorn light-brown hair, the fingers of his other hand probing the purpling discoloration of his jaw. His knuckles are bruised, the skin broken across his second and third joint. He shoots a steely glare as he tongues his split lip, one side slightly puffed where the flesh has ripped.

West and the last guy are sharing a joke, and from the bits I gather of their conversation, they're quietly discussing my kicking the king's ass a few weeks ago. This guy is the biggest of them all: easily six foot seven or eight, with a full-scale lumberjack beard. He's built wide and sturdy, with thick arms and thighs, black hair, cut close to his nape and left shaggy on top. His deep laugh resonates throughout the room.

A sense of loneliness fills me, even in the throng of people. An unfortunate realization dawns, that with Rhys across the room, I feel more alone than I have in a very long time.

Ain't this a kick in the teeth.

I'm nursing the beer West slung my way when I sat down, contemplating how vile I think hops are, when the hot, suit-wearing, Portuguese-speaking man approaches. His posture is friendly and unassuming, and while he's smiling, I get no hint he's trying to flirt.

"I'm Carver Lee," he introduces himself, thrusting out his hand to shake.

"Aurelia Constantine," I say as I take his palm in a sure grip.

Many years ago, I would turn my fingers in his like the lady my mother wished I'd been. But I've found people take you seriously when you give a good hand-shake—not too soft or people think you're weak, not too hard or people think you're an asshole. His grip is firm without being rude.

"Pleased to meet you. Have you been introduced to the rest of these bastards, or are you running blind?"

I'm never blind. I fought hard for these eyes.

"Blind as a bat," I say demurely, lying my ass off.

I'm trying exceptionally hard to say the bare minimum. I don't know if these men are my friends or enemies, and given my track record, I have every right to be wary. The only person I can trust completely is myself. My gut says they are on my side, but any one of these gentlemen could be swayed.

It doesn't take much.

My parents taught me that.

"Allow me, then. This is my husband, Javier Cabal." He gestures to his companion on the couch, and Javier salutes with two fingers. "The two jolly bastards playing pool are Aidan Keenan and his brother, Ian Moran. Aidan is the one wearing the beanie like a twenty-year-old hipster." This earns him the finger from the beanie-wearing man himself.

"The two crybabies pouting on the couch are Cameron O'Connor and Asher Crane. Asher won, by the way," he says as an aside behind his hand, but Cameron seems to hear him, his battered face pulling in a distorted frown. "And last but not least, this big son of a bitch is Kyle Brennan." He slaps the giant man on the shoulder.

"You sure are being awfully nice to someone who kicked the crap out of your king. Should I expect an ambush later?" I say more to myself than anything, but he answers me.

"You and I both know you only won because he let you. Games are afoot, my dear, and they don't stop just because you call a timeout. But war's a funny thing—you gotta make friends where you can."

Coyly tilting my head to the side, I ask, "And I'm a friend?"

"No. But you're not an enemy." He taps his lips like he's trying to decide. "Let's call it an acquaintance with the option for friendship."

"How very lawyerly of you," I grouse, rolling my

eyes. "I can agree to that. I take it that's your Jag outside."

"Well, it's no fair playing guessing games with a seer." He straightens the knot of his tie before brushing invisible lint from his shoulders. "Did my impeccable fashion sense give me away?"

"Absolutely." *Yeah, we'll go with that.*

He narrows his eyes a smidge, likely irritated by my vague answers. "You don't talk much, do you?"

"The line between intelligence and stupidity is easily crossed with an open mouth." I shoot him my most saccharine smile.

"Too right. Take these poor bastards over here"—He gestures to the pouty men sitting on the couch like scolded children—"filled with piss and vinegar over a mere difference of opinion."

"And that would be?"

Carver pauses, and I see the debate play out behind his eyes before he answers me.

"You know, it's so trivial, I've already forgotten," he lies with a careless flick of his wrist. "Perhaps a bit of nonsense over a girl."

My head tilts to the side without thought, and my eyes glow without anger, their reflected light shining off his cufflinks. Knowledge streams into my brain, confirming that Carver is evading my questions to the point of lying.

I really hate being lied to.

Especially since the fight was about me and Rhys staying here. But why? Are we more of a danger to them than I thought? Am I not amongst friends?

The whole room tenses at the pale light shining from my eyes, and Rhys is already crossing the room. He's in front of me before I can blink, a vicious growl bubbling from his throat, his shoulders tensed and ready to strike.

Gently, I rest my hand on Rhys' back, doing my best to calm him because a Phoenix vs. Wraith cage-match is not what we need right now. He startles as if being touched by a tender hand is a foreign concept. As if he's never felt a soothing gesture in his whole life.

Maybe he hasn't.

"I think it's time for bed," I suggest, forcing him to meet my gaze. "Rhys, walk me to the room, won't you?"

He grabs my hand and tugs me toward the staircase.

"Oh, Carver," I call out sweetly, tilting my head over my shoulder as we reach the third step.

"Yes?" His wary voice is telling. He knows he fucked up.

"That's strike one. You lose your options for friend-ship when you lie to me."

7

AURELIA

Rhys drops my hand as soon as we top the stairs, leading me to our room, likely for lack of something better to do. Waiting until our door is closed, he asks the question he's probably been dying to ask the entire trek but couldn't.

"What did you see?"

Debating on what to tell him, I fiddle with the bracelets on my wrist. I must stall too long because he puts a hand over the silver to silence them.

"Tell me."

"The two men who look like they beat the shit out of each other? Carver lied to me about what their fight was about. It wasn't anything major, it's just... everyone's on edge. Wraiths have been attacked in the surrounding areas and then the show gets attacked…" I shrug, pulling my hand from his—gently this time. "I'm picking up on everyone's tension. It's probably nothing. We're safe here."

Rhys sighs before dropping to the edge of the bed, clearly surveying the overdone romance shtick. He doesn't meet my eyes, either embarrassed that Evan did this, or something else I can't name.

"I can sleep on the floor if you want," he offers in a gruff whisper.

A part of me hurts that he felt like he had to suggest the option—that being next to me brings him just as much pain as it does to me.

Deciding to be a full-fledged grown up, I answer him: "Don't worry about it. We could both probably starfish on that bed and not touch. Don't suffer on my account."

Don't suffer on my account. That sentence zings through me as I head to the bathroom to get ready for bed.

How long has he been suffering? I wonder. And how much of it is because of me?

I have a sneaking suspicion the answer is "Always" and "All of it."

My screams have quieted now. I lost my voice what seems like hours ago. The tears have yet to dry, but as long as there is blood in my veins, there will be tears in my eyes. In my throat. On my skin.

Lucien's body is cold in my embrace, long since dead. I adjust my grip on him, wrapping my arms tighter around his shoulders, grasping him to me, trying to hold his soul a little longer. Our blood has mixed and mingled, soaked into the threads of my dress. I tried wiping the blood from his lips, but it only smeared, his skin refusing to come clean.

It's getting harder to hold him now.

Harder to think.

Harder to breathe.

I ache down to my bones. So tired. I need a healer, but the more I think about it, the more I wish no one would come to my rescue. My whole family is dead on this forest floor. The ones who used to call themselves blood turned their backs on us. Lucien and our child were all I had left after my parents' betrayal.

I have nothing now.

Rhys left hours ago. Searching for help maybe? Perhaps he'll die in the forest like I wish I would.

If I were gone from this earth, maybe Lucian, our unborn

child, and I would be together on the Otherside. But I know Lucien would hate to see me so weak, giving up on life so soon—even if dying would be a relief.

My beautiful, strong husband. I thought we would have more time.

The leaves beneath us are as dry as kindling, and before the thought can finish its path in my mind, my fingers have already ignited them. I watch the foliage curl, praying the flames would harm instead of heal.

But they don't.

Carefully, I slide Lucien from my lap to the ground, brushing his golden locks from his bloodstained face—the face that once held so much laughter, so much love. Another soundless sob erupts from my throat as I lay my fiery hand upon his chest. I wish I had enough knowledge of the funeral rites to do this the proper way.

But I know enough. Enough to send him on.

I caress his cheek, his shirt, his trousers, his body igniting as I go, turning the forest floor into his funeral pyre. I still cannot stand—the wound at my belly continues to ooze blood. So there I sit next to his burning body, my tears drying in the heat of the flames before they ever reach my cheeks.

This is where they find me. One hand on the knife that took my husband and child from me, and the other buried in Lucien's ashes.

Phased and flaming, broken and tattered.

Gunning for vengeance and ready for death.
But death...
Death is not what I got.

FOR THE FIRST TIME IN FOREVER, I WAKE UP SCREAMING. THE electricity under my skin is bubbling up and out, flickering to nothing as soon as I realize I'm awake. With the pulse I sent out, I've blown out the lamps and bedside clock, and the television mounted over the fireplace is smoking. The bed curtains are singed, but not on fire, and the linens appear to be unharmed. The only light comes through the open bathroom and hallway doors.

I'm alone until Rhys runs in from the bathroom with a small red cylinder in his hands, squirting white foam on the TV.

A fire extinguisher?

How many years has it been since I've set something on fire in my sleep? Fifty? A hundred?

My vision is wobbly, and I can't stop shaking. With a *thunk*, Rhys drops the extinguisher on the floor by the edge of the bed. His warm hands reach for me, slowly cupping my shoulders. He doesn't say anything, but I can't blame him.

I wouldn't know what to say, either.

"Don't. Don't touch me," I croak, my eyes rolling in my head like a spooked horse.

His hands not only don't go away, but they wrap around me and pull me into a hug. It's soft and warm and comforting, and for a few seconds, I relax in his embrace. But after all I remember, after all the guilt weighing down my soul, the feeling of his chest against my cheek is enough to make me lose my mind.

Instead of comfort, now all I feel are the cold, hard hands that tore at my flesh. The ones who pulled the skin from my bones. The ones who tortured me for what seemed like an eternity. Funny how that eternity had only been three days.

And that's when I start clawing and shrieking like a feral cat.

"Let me go. Let. Me. *Go*," I screech as I scratch, punch, and kick my way free, many of the blows unnecessary since he let me go almost instantly.

Scrambling backward across the bed, I half-step, half-fall off the other side.

I know that time in my life is over. I know it was a long time ago. But I still feel those fucking phantom hands on me even now.

Focus! Focus, dammit!

I clutch my head, my fingers digging into the flesh of

my scalp. And while I can't feel the bite of my nails breaking the skin, Rhys can because he hisses in response. He crosses the room, grabbing my wrists, gently pulling them down and away.

"Stop. You have to stop, Aurelia," he murmurs as I try to get my mind back to the here and now.

I must not have been very successful because he's roaring for Evan.

Soon, our room is invaded by one pissed-off baby wraith, her hands black as coal smoke and curled into talons. The iris and sclera of her usually ice-blue eyes have bled to an almost-demonic black, and she's hissing like a snake through a set of impressive fangs.

Holy shit balls.

That's enough to scare anyone straight, or at least shock me enough to get my shit together. Even with bullets flying in the gallery, Evan didn't fully phase. I'd almost forgotten how scary she could be.

"Put the fangs away, baby doll," I croak. "It's just a flashback."

Just as the words leave my mouth, a very relieved Rhys pulls me into a bone-crushing hug. His embrace is tight enough to steal my breath and warm enough to calm me down to almost normal—or as normal as I'm ever going to get.

"Sorry, guys. Where's a straitjacket when you need

one, huh?" I say on a self-deprecating chuckle as I gently push away from Rhys.

He lets me go this time, and I realize I'm wearing next to nothing by way of a loose T-shirt and underwear. That, and the door is open to all and motherfucking sundry with nine warriors peering inside this room.

Fuck. My. Life.

Running to the bathroom like my ass is on fire, I shut the door with a hearty slam. And thank the Fates for forethought, because my duffle is on the vanity. Showering for the second time in twenty-four hours, I sluice off the spent adrenaline and fear. It takes time to rub the blood from my scalp, but the small crescent wounds from my nails nearly healed already.

Staring down at my arms, and through the ink, I spot the slight ridges of scars covered by beautiful pictures. Koi-like mermaids swimming toward a lotus flower conceal a few. Beautiful dark-haired women in *Dia de Los Muertos* makeup hide others. There are flowers and sea creatures and quotes from my favorite novels and songs. An intricate butterfly covers a jagged scar on my ribs. No matter how I treated it, it never healed properly. A cherry blossom tree conceals the thin scar on my abdomen Rhys and I most likely share.

I remember every single second of my time in that

hell. I remember every single cut Iva and her soldiers sliced into my skin, making them permanent with those stupid knives. And Morganite is supposed to mean true love.

True love my ass.

I took those horrible scars and turned them into something better. My tattoos made something ugly and twisted pretty again. Just like my soul, every prick of the needle healed my flesh, took what was dirty and made it new. I'm better than I was before. I'm stronger. And I won't be defeated by some fucking flashback.

I will not falter.

I refuse.

Dressing in workout clothes, I finish by pulling my hair into a messy knot on top of my head. I grab my phone and earbuds and set my shoulders, praying no one is in the room when I head out.

I should have known that I've never been that lucky.

Rhys is sitting on the bed, much like he did last night—nervous and riled, trying to figure out what to say and failing miserably. He opens his mouth only to close it with a snap as he anxiously runs a hand through his hair.

"Out with it," I bark, because I've been standing here for five full minutes waiting for him to get his shit together enough to spill.

"What was your dream about?" he asks just above a whisper. "Was it a vision? What did you see that made you scream as if you were being tortured?"

I want to feel sorry for him—to comfort him a little —but a bigger, harder part of me wants him to pay for the pain he caused. The gentleness I felt for him last night is long gone.

Why did he have to kill Lucien? We were leaving the Legion. Others got to leave. We weren't the first to choose something different. We were *choosing* exile.

He should feel the same pain—he should know what I endured. The cruelest part of me rears her ugly head—the part that allowed me to survive. The awful part that forced me to trudge forward without them.

Alone.

"It wasn't a dream or a vision. It was a flashback. And I *was* being tortured. I was reliving scattering the ashes of my dead husband. The husband you killed. The husband I was putting to rest when Iva's soldiers caught me. And before that, I got to relive the death of my unborn child. So, you see the flash-back itself was torture—those screams were real." I sneer through my tears, but the satisfaction doesn't last.

His expression wounds me more than anything— because I know that look has been on my face more times than I can count. It's the look of misery. Of guilt. Of remorse. And to give that look to someone else?

It tears me up inside.

I'd give anything to take my words back—to have just shut my mouth and never said anything at all. I part my lips to tell him I didn't mean it, but he's already up from the bed and out the door, the slam of the wood ricocheting through my chest.

Gritting my teeth, I swallow down the sob that tries to break free. I'm getting so fucking sick of how much the guilt of hurting him burns.

I didn't kill anyone. *I* didn't ruin his life.

He ruined mine.

So why does hurting him hurt me so badly?

Yes, we're bonded, but I can't remember when I started giving a shit about breaking his heart. How long has it been? And how long have I been fighting myself— fighting him—making us both miserable in the process?

Sniffing back my tears, I rub the wetness from my cheeks as the anger builds. I want to hit something, but the person I want to hit the most is unavailable to me. As pissed as I am, I quickly realize I haven't eaten in at least twelve hours, and I could eat a moose if my palatal inclinations swung that way.

And that bullshit pisses me off, too.

Opening the door, I make sure the coast is clear

before heading downstairs to raid the fridge. I know wraiths have some wonky eating habits, but there's bound to be food somewhere in this place.

The kitchen walls are a mix of planked wood and horizontal logs, a hearty stone backsplash that mesh perfectly with the granite countertops. The Viking stove sits directly across from a copper sink big enough to bathe in. I crack open the monster of a refrigerator and hit the motherload.

Leftover steak and potatoes, a huge bowl of salad, and a small vat of mixed fruit all get pulled out and devoured before I can stop myself. I'm still angry, but at least I'm marginally sated. I rinse my dishes and load them into the dishwasher to be a somewhat decent houseguest.

I turn to head back to my room, but before I can make it a step, Evan appears right in front of me in a swirl of black smoke.

"Dick move, dude," I hiss, clutching at my chest. "Quit popping up all over the place. It's a house, not a continent. You can walk, you know."

"Don't sass me, Ari," she gripes, her fists making a home for themselves on her hips. "What the fuck is wrong with you?"

No doubt Rhys tattled on me.

"What's wrong with me? What the fuck is wrong

with *you*? I have a fucking flashback, and because you have me roomed with Rhys—and don't think we're not going to have a lengthy, in-depth discussion about that shit—he freaks out watching me recover and starts asking questions. *Of course* I ripped his head off. *Of course* I'm contrary and mean. If you had to relive the worst day of your life, you would be, too. And what was with you appearing in a full-fledged phase? And the dudes just watching me go full monkey shit? I need some privacy. I don't need to be looked at like I'm a freak when I have a breakdown—which I have regularly, or did you forget? I need to hit something that's not going to hurt me when I hit it, and I need to get the *hell* out of *here*."

This is too much for me. I live alone for a reason.

"I had to room you with him—it's Dad's rule," she says remorsefully, but I'm not buying it.

"Oh, whatever," I argue. "You're only using that as an excuse to screw West under your dad's roof. Don't lie to me."

"Yes, that's a perk, but seriously, it's Dad's rule. A guardian can't protect someone he's not with."

"And when the king speaks…" I mutter on a sigh.

"You nod and smile and do what he says. Exactly. I'm sorry this is so hard on you, but you have to cut Rhys some slack. There are things you don't know. Things I can't tell you… things that could change how you see him."

"Cryptic much?" I grunt out with a half-muffled laugh.

"Hey, I tell you what I can, and hold your fucking hand and show you the rest. Just ask him to explain," Evan shoots back. "Have you ever asked him why? He'd answer you."

"I know, but…" I trail off, not ready to hear his side of the story.

"But nothing," she growls, her eyes flashing black for just a moment. "*Ask* him."

"That might take a while, and I need to make someone bleed first. Got anyone in mind?" My mind starts reeling just contemplating a serious conversation with Rhys—one where we don't kill each other.

"You really frighten me sometimes." Evan is smiling now, so score one for me.

"You scare the shit out of me, too, kid," I admit, clapping her on the shoulder. "It's why we're besties."

"Touché." She nods, looping her arm around mine and dragging me to the lowest level of the house—or what I *think* is the lowest level.

Evan heads to the back wall of the game room and leads me behind the bar. She fiddles with an expensive bottle of Scotch and presses a hidden button on the mirror behind an empty decanter. Like an old film noir flick, a secret door opens to reveal a dark staircase.

"What the hell is this?" I stare in awe.

"You said you wanted to hit something. There's a whole training center in the basement full of hot, sweaty men just waiting to get a crack at the girl who kicked their king's ass."

"Wonderful," I deadpan, not too eager to traverse those stairs now that I know what's awaiting me down there.

"Don't say I never did anything for you."

8

AURELIA

SILENTLY, WE MAKE OUR WAY DOWN THREE STEEL FLIGHTS OF stairs, leading to an open room, lit by several industrial pendant lights. The room appears to be used as a sparring and lifting gym and seems to be twice the width and height of the house above it, and maybe three times the length.

In the far-left corner is a boxing ring. Five red ropes surround the elevated platform, and Rhys and West are circling each other on the canvas like rabid dogs. West is shirtless, soaked in sweat, his hair up in a man-bun with stray hairs falling into his eyes. His loose, black Gi pants hang off his hips in such a way that one wrong move could turn this sparring session into a full show.

His nose is bloody, his left eye a little swollen, but other-wise, he doesn't look too bad considering how hard Rhys is hitting him.

I cock my head to the side to get a better view of his ass.

"You know, he's not bad looking with the tattoos and gauges and shirtless and sweaty and those pants..." I shift to face Evan in admiration. "You did good, kid."

"I know. He's yummy, isn't he? I guess I'll keep him. Rhys isn't bad looking, either. You could—"

I pinch her lips together to shut her up. "Already angry. Let's not push me over the edge just yet. Let me hit something first."

Suddenly, I taste the tang of blood and my nose starts to drip. I wipe beneath my nostrils, and my fingers come away red. West must have gotten in a hit hard enough to make Rhys bleed.

Rude.

But my gaze strays back to the ring. Rhys is covered neck to wrists in a blue compression workout shirt, paired with loose black workout shorts, his hands covered in lightly padded, fingered sparring gloves. His nose is just as bloody as mine, his upper lip stained red.

Rhys' moves are economical and calculated—for every step West takes, he has a counter. For every strike with a leg, there is a back-fist or an elbow. They aren't playing by any rulebook that I know of—their style is more like "anything goes" mixed with dirty street fighting. Neither seem to want to grapple, and even when one of them is open for a takedown, the other appears unwilling to take the bait, making the sparring session go on and on.

To the right of the ring is a swinging, red heavy bag, hanging from the concrete wall. Javier— his hands in black wraps—is pounding the bag hard enough to make it sway almost off the hook. His hair and skin are damp with sweat, and every once in a while, he picks up the T-shirt draped over a nearby metal folding chair to wipe the salt off his face.

Carver is right next to him on the speed bag—hands in white wraps—hitting the bag faster than my eyes can track. His lean build is cut with diamond-hard muscle, barely covered in a sleeveless workout shirt.

Along the right wall are three sections of lifting platforms. The first one seems to be used for dumbbells and kettlebells, while the second and third belong to the two side-by-side squat racks laden down with enough weights to sink a ship. At the last rack, Kyle is setting up for a lift that would crush a rhinoceros, his damp hair falling into his eyes.

On the near-right wall is a sea of pegboards, and the adjacent surface is covered in the handholds of a climbing wall. Why an indoor climbing wall is necessary with a whole fucking mountain outside, is anyone's guess. Aidan is fifty feet above us—at the top of the board—with a peg in each hand. As he goes to wipe his brow on the sleeve of his compression shirt, his hand slips from its hold on the dowel, and like a fucking moron, he's not tied into the safety ropes hanging intermittently from the ceiling rafters. He begins to fall, but swiftly smokes out from his rapid descent and is back at the top in his original position, no worse for wear.

Okay, maybe he's *not* a moron.

Ian is appropriately tied into a climbing harness hooked up to a self-belay system in the rafters. It occurs to me that the reason he's tied in and Aidan isn't is because Ian can't transport himself like the other wraiths can. How odd. Maybe he's young or doesn't possess that particular ability.

That, I completely understand.

While I might have wings, they are utterly useless. Not only did I *not* learn how to fly—*thanks, Mom*—Iva permanently clipped my wings when she tortured me.

I swear if I ever meet that woman again, I'm going to cut her fucking head off.

In the largest area at the middle of the room is an immense sparring mat. The thick, blue canvas spans approximately fifty feet wide and one hundred feet long, offset by the substantial collection of weapons affixed to the adjacent wall. The "Wall 'O Weapons" includes every bladed instrument I can think of and some I haven't seen in nearly a century.

"So heavy bag, weights, climbing wall, or the mat?" Evan ticks off our options on her fingers.

"Mat," I tell her, but I notice West has stopped messing around with Rhys and is leaning on the ropes.

His body is coiled in such a way, if I suggest sparring with my best friend, he'll launch himself over those ropes before I can blink. I meet his gaze, shaking my head. I won't spar with his little bird, no matter how likely it would be that she'd kick my ass.

It makes me wonder if he even has a clue that we used to spar on the regular. Evan's keeping more secrets than I can count. I hope she knows what she's doing.

"I'm going to do a few training exercises by myself. Katas can be done alone, you know. Go cheer your man on. Tell him to show no mercy."

She quirks a brow. "He's giving you the evil-eye stare down, isn't he?"

"Absolutely." I nod emphatically. "I'm positive if I touch a hair on your beautiful blonde head, he'll try to kill me in a way I won't heal from. No offense, babe, but I really don't want a showdown with your boyfriend. As much as I love you, I think I need a new sparring partner."

She pivots on a heel and sticks her tongue out at the man in question. *"Fun killer."*

His stoic mask slips for a second, and a wide grin flashes across his face before quickly disappearing.

"Go watch the boys beat the shit out of each other. I'm fine by myself."

"Have fun," she says as she skips toward the ring.

Even from across the room, I notice as West's face softens a fraction before returning to Rhys with renewed fervor brought on by the presence of his girl. Maybe he'll break Rhys' neck, and I'll get a nice dreamless nap.

Pulling out my phone, I choose the perfect song from my "Pissed Off" playlist, stuff my earbuds in my ears, and set my phone on the hard rubber floor. Selecting a short red-oak bokken from the wall, I bow to the mat and begin.

By the time I'm done with my fifth song, "Joker and the Thief" by Wolfmother starts, and I finally look up. I'm sweaty and a little tired, but I notice I've drawn a crowd. A trill of unease races up my spine. I'm still going through the movements, but I'm aware of my surroundings now.

I feel like my ass is in a bear trap—teeth on all sides.

West, Carver, and Javier are at the edge of the mat closest to me, still respectfully off the canvas, their feet bare like mine. Aidan, Ian, and Kyle are in shoes—on the motherfucking mat—and walking closer. With all these weapons, you'd think everyone would have the respect required for *the mat*, but I guess not. Pausing slightly, I flick an earbud from my ear as I wait for the catch in a breath that will telegraph an impending movement.

It comes from Kyle.

The big man moves faster than expected—especially with the bulk he has—but he's not fast enough. I'm three feet away from my original position, and his big fingers clutch only air. Aidan strikes next, smoking out and popping up six inches away from where I used to be, but now he has a stinging ass cheek where my bokken struck him like a naughty child. Ian just stands there with his hands in his pockets—a sign of peace more than anything else—before turning and walking off the mat as he smiles and shakes his head.

I still don't trust him, but he's less of a threat right now. I pivot to face my intruders.

Kyle and Aidan must have some wordless communication down because they move as one—Kyle running and Aidan popping out simultaneously. Aidan reaches me first, but instead, gets the nasty surprise of my bokken upside his skull. He stumbles, landing on his hands and knees, shaking off the strike to his temple. Before Kyle can get within touching distance, I sweep his legs out from under him with my practice sword.

A shuffling of feet at my back ignites my rage. "You have less than a second to stop and get your dirty, disrespectful shoes off this fucking mat. If I have to tell you twice, you'll regret it."

"Aww. But it was just starting to get fun." Ian chuckles as he picks his brother up off the mat.

Aidan appears a little green around the gills as he passes, his arm thrown over Ian's shoulder. Maybe I hit him harder than I thought. *Oops.*

Maybe next time he won't use his abilities in a sparring session.

Kyle's still on his back, looking dazed and confused.

"You all right?" I ask, glancing over at the felled giant.

"Yeah," he groans. "How'd you do that?"

The sheer disbelief in his tone makes me giggle. "What? Kick your ass?"

"Yeah." He chuckles breathlessly. "That."

"Three ways," I reply, ticking off my index finger. "One, I'm really good at reading people, and you telegraph your movements about half a second before you strike. You may wanna work on that."

He cocks his head and squints one eye as he

attempts to focus on my face. "So noted. And the second?"

I tick off my middle finger. "I train every. Single. Day."

That raises his eyebrows, and lifts his head as he incredulously asks: "Why?"

"Because a long time ago, I didn't have the luxury. And it cost me. Dearly," I answer as I level my gaze with his, sobering him instantly.

"And the third?" he croaks.

"I'm a fucking psychic, you dumbass," I tell him, rolling my eyes as I shake my head at the sheer stupidity housed in a single person.

"Huh. I didn't know you were an oracle. How come you still have your eyes?"

"I'm not an oracle," I mutter, massaging my temples, praying for patience. "Just a lowly little seer on the run from her Legion. I like my eyes parked exactly where they are—even if they are ugly as sin."

"Valid." He waggles his eyebrows at me. "Wanna help me up?"

"You still planning on pulling me down? 'Cause ground tactics aren't going to work so well for you when I fry your ass from the inside out."

He purses his lips in contemplation. "I think I'll get myself up."

"Good plan," I mutter as the big man slowly pulls himself to standing, hobbling off the mat.

West and Javier bow to the canvas, then to each other, and start sparring on the far end. They are doing a light-touch technique that focuses more on control of movements rather than strikes.

Carver starts clapping slowly, and I use the bokken like a cane, performing a little bow before stowing the sword on its pegs and moving out of the way.

"Enjoy the show?"

"Immensely," he purrs. "You know they were just playing, right? They wouldn't hurt you."

"Because I'm a girl?" I ask incredulously.

"Because their king has offered you his protection. They only wanted to see what you were made of."

"And here I went easy on them. If I had known it was a dog and pony show, I would have shown some of my best tricks."

"Don't be a snot, dear," he derides with a scoff. "It's unbecoming."

"Don't be condescending," I growl. "It's rude."

"Touché. So what happened this morning? I thought we were getting ready for a fight, and it turns out, you blew up your room. People were phased, shit was on fire." He shoots me a bewildered side-eye. "What the fuck, girlie?"

I shrug, trying to think of a way to explain the drama without sounding like a complete fucking nutter. There isn't.

Might as well go with the truth.

"Well. I have dreams. Sometimes they're visions and sometimes they're flashbacks. Either way, they make me completely batshit crazy. On occasion, I wake up screaming my head off and setting shit on fire by accident. Rhys is not familiar with my episodes, so there was a"—I pause, holding up my fingers spaced ever so slightly apart—"*misunderstanding* this morning."

"So, you're telling me he was yelling the house down because he was worried about you?"

Pursing my lips, I nod. "Essentially."

"And this is a problem because...?"

Oh, the can of worms the honesty would open.

Wincing, the crux of the matter ekes past my lips. "We have a history and it's not pleasant."

"Don't we all? Maybe, since he gives a shit and all, you should cut him some slack? Friends are hard to come by."

Sage advice. Too bad it's easier said than done.

"You're not the first person to tell me that today."

"So, if enough people say it to you, you'll actually believe it? Because I've been watching you two, and whatever you're carrying? It's hurting you both."

9

RHYS—1855

HELPLESSLY, I TENSED AS I WATCHED MY BROTHER ARM himself. When he'd first told me of his mission three days ago, I stood there in shock. His face was so animated and joyful as he calmly discussed the planned assassination of a woman who had done nothing wrong.

I'd always thought phoenixes were indestructible. My parents dying so unexpectedly convinced me we were not. The right blade in the wrong hands could steal our lives just as easily as a human's.

We were supposed to be good, meant to keep the balance—to ferry souls on to be reborn.

Never to fight.

Never to steal life.

Where Julian lost his way, I hadn't a clue.

Only ten years my senior, he'd known our parents better than I ever had, but I remembered them well enough. They never would have allowed something like this. I'd been fifteen years old when our parents were killed—the circumstances of which were still a mystery. We never got the full story from Iva or the head families. We never got to put them to rest. One day they were here, and the next we'd become orphans.

Overnight, Julian became my only family, and then he started to change.

It wasn't the metamorphosis of a man losing his loved ones. It was the change of a man losing his mind. Brick by brick, stone by stone, everything that had once been my fun, good-natured brother was lost as soon as he became a soldier.

But tonight was different.

It wasn't until I'd become a soldier myself, that I realized just how wrong everything we'd been told actually was—how wrong Julian was.

Tonight he armed himself—not to protect but to murder. All because our Primary told him to.

Taking everything we stood for and throwing it away like garbage.

I tried talking to him—tried getting him to see

reason—until I realized what I had to do as soon as the word "kill" passed his lips.

I only hoped I had the courage to do it.

"Jules?" I called as we walked from our modest house into the neighboring forest, staying on the path that led to a steep cliff.

"What is it, Rhys?" he barked as he adjusted his blades, picking up the pace. "I don't have much time."

It was now or never.

"I want to go with you," I lied, hoping he didn't see through me. "Keep an eye out for you. This isn't what we usually do. I'm worried."

As his little brother, I always tagged along, so my behavior could be attributed to that instead of my real purpose—being a Judas.

His steps stuttered, and he glanced back at me, relief instantly washing over his face. "Sure, little brother. I'd love to have you with me."

His easy agreement was worse than a knife to the gut.

Because the relief I heard in his voice hadn't been because I was coming with him or that I accepted his mission. It was because I was falling in line. He'd been worried he might have to end me because of my behavior.

Because I wouldn't conform.

I forced a tremulous smile as I waited for the ache in my chest to ease. "Jules, did they ever tell you why? I understand following orders, but this is so far out of our norm..." I trailed off as he turned back to me, leveling me with a single venomous glance.

"I don't need to know why, Rhys," he hissed on a harsh whisper, as if someone might hear him on this secluded hilltop. "It is not my place to know. It isn't yours either."

The brother I knew was truly gone. My eyes stung with the tears of a boy who had just lost the last of his family.

"I understand, brother," I whispered, plodding along behind him as my stomach churned.

Managing to keep my emotions at bay, the loss still dug deep into my chest. Julian—the same brother who tended to me when I broke my arm falling from a tree, the one who played with me when our parents were busy with the council, the one who would pick family over his friends at the drop of a hat—was now lost to me.

He felt different. He felt evil. I knew it in my soul—this wasn't the first life he would take, and if I didn't stop him, it wouldn't be the last.

We made it to the edge of the cliff and phased in an instant—Julian much faster than I—spread our wings and soared from the precipice, the wind roaring in our ears and kissing our cheeks.

The freedom I desired never came.

I felt worse than numb—I was dead inside.

Because my brother had to be stopped—he had to. Julian didn't care that he was blithely running off to kill someone. It didn't matter if it was a woman, and he didn't even have the decency to ask why.

He honestly didn't care.

Our destination was remote: a modest log cabin no more than fifty miles north. We landed in the thick of the forest a few miles from the house and waited for the full cover of night.

I wanted to hug him—to reminisce about the good times—but I didn't. If I did, I wouldn't follow through.

When the moon finally made her appearance, Julian stood, marching at a quick clip in the direction of the cabin. He didn't even make it to the trees before a large man formed—seemingly from the darkness—right in his path.

The stranger was tall with midnight hair pulled away from his face in a leather thong. His features seemed worse than deadly, which at that point, was not the best feeling in the world.

He looked past my shocked brother and asked, "You Rhys?"

"Yes. This is Julian, my brother. He plans to kill your queen," I confessed on a whisper, but I had no doubt they heard me.

Julian shifted to face me, betrayal stamped all over his features.

"We are not made to kill innocents, brother," I murmured, my voice laced with the apology I could never give. "I can't let you murder someone."

I couldn't give it because I wasn't sorry. My only regret was losing the very last person I could call family.

"You can choose," the man I knew only as West offered Julian. "Leave with your brother or die here with me. Either way, you aren't getting past me, child. I'll let you go, but if you take another step toward that house, I'll kill you before you can take another breath."

My brother didn't hesitate, moving like a lightning strike toward West, but the wraith was faster. Julian's neck was snapped in an instant, his inert body falling to the dirt.

"That way won't kill us, you know," I croaked. I tried to keep the sorrow from my voice, but I was unsuccessful. "He'll come back."

"Oh, I know," West muttered gently, the compassion in his voice more than I could take. "I just didn't plan on killing your brother in front of you."

"Thank you," I whispered, unable to bring my voice any louder.

"You're doing the right thing, and as soon as you name it, you may call on any favor from the king," West promised, giving me a slight bow of his head before grabbing my brother's hand and disappearing in a swath of black smoke.

I had a feeling I'd be needing that favor very soon.

I HAD NO PLANS TO GO BACK TO MY LEGION, NO PLANS TO SEE Aurelia's face again—to ever be bound to her.

But my life had been one wrong turn after another. Leaving everything and everyone I knew, I headed toward a secluded cabin in the Canadian Rockies I'd set up before my Selection.

After my parents' death, I didn't trust my Legion, Iva, or my species. I wanted to, sure, but I couldn't—not when my inquiries were met with a bunch of "I don't knows" and "Quit asking questions"—none of which inspired much confidence in a man. So, I did the only thing I knew to do and made a plan—trusting that if I waited and played the long game, I would be fine.

Turned out, I was an idiot.

When daylight crested, I was still in the Oregon territory, my travel hindered by poor night vision and the cold, autumn air. I was tired, and I figured that was the only reason they caught me. Well, that and because I was an absolute moron. Let's not forget that little fact.

Honestly, how much of a fool could I have been? Had I really thought an oracle of the highest order—who would demand the death of an innocent—wouldn't be keeping an eye on the man who was too stupid to stop asking questions?

My parents were dead. I didn't know why, but I was fairly certain who'd ripped them from me. Julian was likely gone, too. The guilt was a knife to the gut.

But I would have preferred the knife of guilt to the red-hot Morganite knife that currently protruded from my belly.

"Once again, Mr. Stevens, do you accept the bond or no?" Iva asked me for the hundredth time, her Irish lilt setting my teeth on edge.

Clad in a long white dress, she appeared like a macabre angel with dark-red splotches of my blood splashed all over her. Her white hair matched her dress, at odds with her youthful face. I didn't know how old she was, only that she'd had plenty of time in her life to learn the art of torture.

She was a master of it.

Each time I said no, I received another slash, another cut, another burn. You'd think phoenixes couldn't burn, but you'd be wrong. When you heated a Morganite knife over an open flame and pressed it against our skin, we burned just like everyone else.

"Well?" she asked as she tossed the bloody blade back and forth between her delicate but deadly hands. "I don't have all day, dearie. It is time to decide. Torture? Or the bond. It isn't the worst thing, you know. Come on, Rhys. Tick tock, dear."

"No," I rasped.

I wouldn't win Aurelia that way. If I agreed to Iva's demands, if I said yes to bonding Aurelia to me… I would be begging her to hate me. Soldier or not, it wouldn't matter if my life would be tied to hers.

If I took away her choices, she would hate me forever.

"Now, now, Rhys. That was the wrong answer," she murmured as she ripped that blade from my gut and ran it from my collarbone past my navel, pressing just enough for the blood to well.

And I screamed for maybe the thousandth time.

"Do. You. Accept?"

I couldn't draw a breath large enough to answer her, so I just shook my head. And it went on and on, again and again. Until I couldn't take another cut or stab or slice or burn.

When I finally said yes, it felt worse than when I handed my brother over to the wraiths.

RHYS

The slow burn of the aged Scotch ignites its way down my throat, setting my stomach on fire. It's 11:00 a.m. on a Wednesday, and I'm sitting in the game room bar with a three-hundred-dollar bottle of Scotch, slowly but surely becoming an alcoholic.

It's been a long time since I've been this angry. Angry enough to fuck up and get myself hit. Angry enough to be a dumb-shit and get her nose bloodied as well as mine. At least my drinking won't affect her, but the consolation is slight.

Why did I have to ask questions?

She was finally warming up to me. She was hugging me, for fuck's sake. She practically slept wrapped around me last night—not that I'd tell her that. But no, I had to go and lose what little ground I had by pushing.

I know who she was dreaming about. And I know how bad it must have been for her, wounded and in agony, lighting Lucien's funeral pyre. He was my friend once, so many years ago. Before I became a soldier.

Before he fell in love with Aurelia. Before he used her to get back at me for a destiny I could never have changed.

Before Iva made me choose between my old friend and the life of the woman I loved. I'll never regret choosing her—even if killing him put a black stain on my soul.

It wasn't the first black mark to reside there.

Lucien had been a good man. Flawed, surely, but he was honorable. And I knew he loved her. But Iva has her ways. That miserable bitch has enough tricks up her sleeve to turn any self-respecting person into her little puppet.

I tried not to hurt him, but whatever Iva did to him —whatever spell she used—turned my once-mild-mannered friend into a crazed, knife-wielding psychopath. I don't think Lucien had touched a blade since we were children—even then, we'd only prac-ticed with wooden swords, pretending to be soldiers. He preferred books—or at least he pretended to—making the scholar position he so loathed into his hobby.

Spinning the tumbler in the growing condensation pooling on the bar top, I study the amber liquid swirling in the glass as it melts the ice. Suddenly, the wall opens to the staircase beyond, and a freshly showered Aurelia and Carver emerge from the hidden door. Facing her right now would be too much for me to bear, so I rotate on my stool, nabbing the bottle as I leave the room.

I wish I knew how long we were going to stay holed up here. Don't get me wrong, the house is amazing, the food is amazing, the people... *blah, blah, blah*. It's all fucking Jim-dandy, but what are we doing here?

John is stonewalling me, refusing to reveal his sources inside the Legion. Aurelia hates me. I'm ready to dismember Kyle and Aidan for trying to touch her. And if Carver talks to her one more time, I'm going to murder him. I don't give a shit if he *is* gay.

John's waiting for something. What that is, I'm not sure. While the added firepower would be beneficial in keeping Aurelia safe, I'm seriously contemplating kidnapping my charge and getting the fuck out of here.

I take the stairs two at a time, climbing each flight all the way up to the loft. Luckily, it's empty, and I can be pissed off in peace. I have half a mind to steal Aurelia's keys and take her car on a joyride. But she'd figure out a way to torture me without breaking my skin for that infraction.

She's good at that.

Choosing a leather armchair close to the south window, I slump down into it. It's July, but the water is probably still cold from the late season snows and runoff. What I wouldn't give to not be mired down with the anxiety of impending war, and for once, just have a day to breathe easy. Maybe a day on the lake in the middle of summer to go fishing or grill out or anything but be a hamster on this wheel of training to keep busy and waiting for the sky to fall.

Just one damn day.

Footsteps slowly scale the stairs behind me, and I force myself not to react.

"Rhys," Aurelia calls softly.

Sighing through my nose, I shift my gaze from the window in acknowledgment but say nothing. Honestly, I'm afraid whatever comes out of my mouth might set her off, and for the first time, she almost sounds sweet.

"I'm sorry," she whispers.

Leaning back in my chair, the confusion nearly bowls me over. "For what?"

"For blowing up our room. For making you bleed during my PTSD freak-out. For losing my fucking mind. For being a class-A bitch. Pretty much the entire day."

Sipping my drink, I nod. "Apology accepted."

She takes a step back, clearly shocked, and I can't figure out why. Doesn't she know I would do anything for her—even forgive a piddly fire?

"That easy?" she asks, her mouth dropping open. "I don't need to get on my hands and knees and grovel?"

She's joking, but the mental image of Aurelia

crawling naked across a messy bed, flashes across my mind. I almost growl aloud at the thought, my jaw tightening as my eyes go half-mast. Hastily, I look out the window to hide my body's response to the seemingly inane comment, praying she doesn't notice my reaction to a simple sentence.

"Nope," I mutter, proud my voice doesn't break like a damn adolescent.

She sighs, wringing her hands. "Well. Thanks. I'll leave you to it," she murmurs before turning to head back down the stairs.

"Aurelia?" I call as she reaches the third step down.

She pauses, her shoulders tightening. "Yeah?"

"I'm sorry, too."

Those words are laced with every bit of regret I've stored in my soul. Regret for saying yes when I should have died before I accepted a bond she didn't want. Remorse for Lucien, for killing him instead of just breaking his neck. Maybe I could have done it different. Maybe I could have saved him.

Maybe then Aurelia wouldn't be mated to someone she couldn't stand, bonded for eternity to the man who took everything from her.

She nods and, Fates help me, her bottom lip begins to tremble.

How many times have I made her cry? A thousand? A million?

"I-it's going to take a little while for me to forgive you. I know you have your side to the story. I know you have things to tell me, and I've been unwilling to listen. I'm sorry I can't give you better than that, but I'm afraid if I forgive you, I'll have to take the burden of all the guilt I've piled on your shoulders. And I can't bear the weight. I have to blame you, because if I don't, I have to start blaming me, and I won't survive the guilt. So, I'm going to have to hate you a little while longer, if you don't mind," she finishes her speech on a whisper, her voice barely reaching my ears.

The tears have broken free of her lashes, running in rivulets down her cheeks as she swiftly makes her way back down the stairs.

Apparently, just one day is too much to ask for.

IO

AURELIA—1855

THEY CAME FOR ME AFTER I SENT LUCIEN ON TO THE
Otherside. After Rhys left me alone in that forest. After I
called upon my meager knowledge of the funeral rights
and sent Lucien to his rest. While I lost the child in my
belly and slowly bled more and more lifeblood. I'd
wanted to die, but I never wanted this.

Soldiers came, and I fought. I fought so hard, but it
wasn't enough. I was beaten and tortured. Iva loved
hurting me, loved it when she drew any measure of
blood. Realization dawned as to what she was doing.

She was making Rhys bleed through me, torturing
us both for something I'd done. For wanting to leave, for
wanting my own life. I was to blame. I would have felt

sorry for him if he hadn't stolen the life I'd created for myself.

Blood-covered and shackled to a stone table, my body was littered with a hundred tiny cuts, burns, and puncture wounds scored into my skin. I wasn't bleeding anymore, and I supposed that was likely a bad thing.

Nicola had lied. I wouldn't see my daughter free of the Legion. I wouldn't see her breathe or live or smile. I hated her more and more each passing second—even if she wasn't the one who made me bleed. Because she was the one who'd made me hope.

Several times I lost consciousness, so I hadn't a clue how long I'd been stuck in this Hell. It felt like years, decades, centuries of pain, but it was more than likely just days. A commotion echoed outside my cell door, the distinct sound of bones breaking—particularly, a neck snapping. The door opened, and the absolute last person I wanted to see stood at the threshold.

He reached for me, and I scuttled away as far as my shackles would allow. I didn't want his dirty, murdering hands on me.

Rhys' face went from relief to agony as he made his way across the room and gently removed my bonds. His hands were soft, but I didn't want them anywhere near me.

"Don't touch me," I rasped, my breath catching in my lungs.

"As soon as I get you safe, you will never have to see me again."

"Good," I whispered as he picked me up and carried me into the light.

AURELIA

It takes no time at all to get to our room. And when the fuck did I start thinking of it as "our" room? The bedclothes still in shambles, I head to the linen closet in the bathroom for replacement sheets, dashing the tears from my cheeks on the way.

Of course, I *had* to cry in front of him. Why not? I've already been a basket case and a bitch today. Why not add in an emotional train wreck and round out the trifecta? I snap the sheets on the bed and search for a hamper to toss the soiled ones in. I'm finally rid of them when Rhys slams into the room.

"Why do you blame yourself?" he roars. "Why can't you put the blame on Iva where it belongs?"

Why couldn't he just leave it alone? *Push. Push. Push.* I take a deep breath and finally snap.

"Because she didn't stab him," I grind out, balling my hands into fists. "*You* did."

"And where would we be if I hadn't? I didn't go after him. He came after me. We were already bound. If I let him kill me, you would have died, too. If I let him cut me, you would've bled too."

Rhys tunnels his fingers into his hair and pulls as if he's ready to rip the strands out from the roots.

"What else would you have had me do?" he asks roughly on a parting shot as he stares down at the floor. After I fail to answer him, he slams out of the room for the second time today.

Trembling, I fall back the few inches until my spine hits the frame of the bathroom door. *Shit.*

Before I can get myself together, the door opens again, and he's back—his anger filling the room. He slams the damn thing closed behind him as he plants his feet, his hands in fists at his sides.

"Do you think I wanted to kill him? Do you think I wanted to watch you hate me for the last damn century? Do you think I asked for these fucking scars?" he asks me on a shout as he roughly tugs the collar of his shirt away to reveal thick, white scars against his olive skin. "Do you think I wanted to be tortured for days on end until I said yes to the binding? What makes scars like this on us, Ari? Huh? What makes these scars?"

They start at the middle of his thick, corded neck, disappearing below the dark fabric.

The only thing that could have made those scars permanent is a Morganite knife. It's why I have two full sleeves, why I have so much ink covering the wounds of torture inflicted by Iva's hands. The torture Rhys saved me from.

But no one saved him.

No one stopped his torment until Iva got what she wanted. Tears flow freely down my cheeks, dripping from my chin and down to my chest.

Even though I didn't hear them, his screams of agony echo through my mind. Gritting my teeth, I remember my own screams, my pleas for death. I can't open my mouth enough to respond. If I do, the keening cry caged in my throat will be set free, and I can't...

I can't.

My poor Rhys. What did they do to you?

"I did not ask to be bound to you. I did not ask to tie myself to someone else's woman. I did not ask for this," he grits, pleading for me to understand. "And you piling guilt on me, blaming me for his death, is not right. *Yes*, I feel guilty. *Yes*, I'm sorry he's dead. But I'd do it all over again if it meant I didn't have to kill you. I'd live the last century mired in the guilt of killing him. I'd do it all again if it meant you were breathing."

"But why?" I croak, amazed I can form the words.

An expression of comprehension dawns on his face,

and suddenly, he's not three feet away, he's right there in front of me with my face in his hands. Why does his touch feel like a warm blanket around my soul? Why do his words—his truth—heal me in a way I've been dying for?

Why do I believe every word out of his mouth?

But most of all, why would he choose my safety, my life, my *everything* over his?

"Why what? Why save you? Because I've loved you since I was twelve years old when you told your mother you'd rather eat a pinecone than wear a corset. I loved you when you didn't love me. I loved you when you were married to someone else, when you were pregnant with another man's child. And I loved you even when you hated me. I loved you before we were bound... and I love you still."

Nodding, for once my head empty of all the trash that brings me down every day. Rhys saved me, doing it the only way he knew how—twice, if memory serves. He pulled me from the flames of Iva's torture. He watched out for me for years, shouldering the blame of something he had no control over.

For the first time, I'm able to put my guilt down, the weight of it all leaving my shoulders like a stack of bricks. No regrets, no recriminations. Nothing but him and the feeling of his rough, callused hands cupping my jaw and the tips of his fingers softly scraping my scalp.

Leaning down, Rhys touches his forehead to mine, the barest hint of breath whispering across my skin. The relief of it makes my shoulders sag. Letting it all go—the deaths of Lucien and my unborn child, a century and a half of agony—all of it.

The regret and guilt were the only things standing in the way of the bond, and now that those obstacles are out of the way, all that's left is my tie to Rhys. And I don't know if it's a spell, or if this is what Fate has destined for us.

I don't know if it's real or manufactured.

I'm not even sure I care.

All I know is, Rhys is here, and safe, and in my arms —something I've wanted in the back of my mind for more than a century but would never allow myself to have.

His lips brush mine, sliding back and forth against them as my mouth parts to breathe him in. His scent fills my nose—it's a faint mix of the Scotch he's been sipping, spice, and something altogether Rhys.

Shuddering at that simple touch of his lips, the iron bands of the bond seal around my heart. I wonder if sheer force of will kept the spell at bay for this long.

Was I just too stubborn to let myself love him?

Did I simply need to forgive him?

To forgive myself?

After all this time?

Then he's kissing me for real, his lips softer than I ever imagined. They cradle mine delicately, and then they turn harder, firmer, fiercer as his hands move from my cheeks to my hips to haul me against his chest.

My hands move, too. They fist in the shirt at his waist, pulling, tugging to get him to me. I need him closer. His tongue strokes into my mouth, and the taste—*Fates*—it's as if I was born to kiss him.

Maybe I was.

His hunger makes my belly dip and knot, my skin flushing as my entire body aches with need. I can't get close enough.

His hands burn against my skin as they climb under my shirt, biting into my flesh in the best possible way. The faint tear of fabric reaches my ears just as a tug jostles my arms—and then my shirt is gone. But *his* shirt is still in the way. The problem is quickly remedied when I rip open his button-up like tissue paper at a birthday party. I pull my mouth from his—but just barely—sharing the crackling air between our scarcely parted lips. Opening my eyes, I peer into the rich coffee color of his.

Those eyes are dancing, his face the happiest,

lightest I've ever seen it. I didn't know Rhys could look this free.

But then I glance down, and I'm absolutely horrified. Not because Rhys is ugly—he could never be ugly. He could be missing limbs, his face could be half-gone, and it wouldn't matter—not now, not anymore. I'm appalled at what has been done to this beautiful man.

How much pain he must have endured to keep from breaking my heart.

How could I have blamed him for a century?

How could I have hated him?

He has endured more than his fair share of agony, too.

Scars run the length of his torso, extending into his trousers. Five thick, white lines as wide as a pencil run from his neck down through his pectoral, past his ribs, and through the muscles of his abdomen. Three burns as big as my hand mar his Legion markings on his stomach.

And the last one—that one? I inflicted.

A three-inch scar sits just above his belt, faint compared to the others he's suffered.

He felt the loss of my child. And I never realized...

I've blamed him all this time, and yet, he endured right along with me.

Gasping out a sob, my shaking hand covers the

worst of the burns, pressing in as if to heal the ruined flesh. His skin is warm and alive as I rest my forehead against his heart.

"I'm so sorry," I keen. "It's my fault—all my fault."

"Shh, baby," he insists on a gruff whisper, his hands tilting my face to his. "You didn't do this to me. None of this is on you."

He slants his head, and his lips are once again on mine. I clutch him to me, my fingers digging into his shoulders. And then he pulls me up, his wide, strong hands at my ass, my legs wrapping around his back.

My fingers immediately sift into his hair, pulling his head to the side so I can taste the skin of his neck, his shoulder, softly nibbling at the flesh. He growls at the touch and walks us backward toward the bed. Then he turns, half-dropping me, half-laying me on the mattress, reaching for my shoes and yanking them off with a careless tug.

I sit up, my fingers already working the buckle of his belt. Just as I yank the first button of his jeans, he cups my face again, kissing me with a blistering heat. We fall back onto the mattress, and his mouth moves to my neck, licking, biting, sucking as his body moves over mine. I can't contain the low moan that erupts from my throat.

Reaching into his jeans, I bypass the remaining

buttons and snake my fingers inside his tight boxer briefs. Wrapping my hand around him, I relish the groan that vibrates from his chest. But before I can give him a good stroke, he grabs my hands, pulling my arms above my head and pressing my wrists into the mattress.

"Don't move," he orders, and the command in his voice causes my breath to hitch.

For once, I do as I'm told, leaving my hands right where they are as he runs his callused finger down my arms, over my breasts, down my stomach, and to my jeans. He quickly works the button and zipper, pulling the denim down my legs, along with my underwear.

My patience runs out—my ability to follow orders flying out the window—and I move from my back to my knees, reaching for his jeans.

They have to come off. Right. Now.

I manage to get the denim pushed past his knees, and before he can stop me, I wrap my hand around his impressive cock. Leaning down, I bring him to my lips, sucking his hard length into my mouth as far as I can. I revel in his scent—in the taste of him.

His feral groan vibrates through my whole body, making the wetness between my legs go from damp to flooded. I get maybe three hard sucks before I'm miraculously on my back again, his wide shoulders between my thighs. His rough hands are under my ass—he's devouring me—his tongue at my opening, his lips on my clit, gently tugging on that bundle of nerves.

I'm about to come, and it's too quick.

It took me one hundred and sixty years to get over our shit. I'm not coming in the first ten minutes, dammit.

"You," I gasp, barely able to breathe. "I wanna come with you." Tugging him up my body, I kiss myself off his lips, loving the taste of my wetness on his tongue. His hands leave my ass and go to his cock, running it up and down my slit before notching it at my opening.

Rhys' fevered gaze practically touches me everywhere.

"You want me?" he rumbles, teasing me until I'm ready to beg.

"Please, honey. Please," I plead, and he gives me what I want, driving his thick shaft into me all the way to the hilt.

My moan is drowned out by his fierce growl, and we nearly freeze at the sensation. Then he's moving, thrusting into me hard enough to steal my breath.

And it's good. *So* good.

I wrap my legs around his thighs, moving my hips in time with his thrusts, meeting him stroke for stroke. His right hand burrows under my back, and the left sifts through my hair. And then we're sitting up, my body on top of his, taking his cock deeper, but sweeter—our mouths barely touching.

He turns us, my back once again pressed into the mattress as my release barrels toward me faster than a freight train. Rhys must feel the same intense pressure I do, because his thrusts become faster, rougher, less controlled. Our gazes meet and lock, the power in them enough to send me over the edge, and I come on a strangled moan. Everything inside me tightens, clamping down hard enough to ache, but in the best way.

Rhys' coffee-colored eyes narrow into slits, and he grits his teeth, coming on a groan, his fingertips digging into my thigh hard enough to bruise, but I don't care. The bite of pain at the end is enough to make my sex spasm around his cock in aftershocks.

His lips find mine again—hard and passionate. He gently pulls out of me and rests his head on my chest, his hard breaths tickling the skin of my breast.

"I love you too, you know," I whisper, confessing this truth for the first time out loud.

Because it's true. I love him, and I'm only just now figuring out that I've loved him for a very long time.

Before Lucien.

Before Rhys saved me.

Before it all went to shit.

I just wouldn't let myself believe it—too stubborn to admit I cared for the man chosen for me.

Well, I'm choosing him now.

"I know. I was just waiting for you to come around," he says with a relieved smile. "I knew you'd get it eventually."

He questioned it, and my declaration moved a weight off his chest. I wonder how many bricks he still had weighing him down.

"Good you know me so well, then," I mutter, rolling my eyes at the gauzy fabric draped over the canopy bed.

"I'm sure there's more to know. It might take me a while—maybe forever—to learn everything. Mind me sticking around?"

It's how he phrased it that kills me—like he's begging for this to be real, praying that what we have isn't just a fluke or a dream or...

I pull his head up and stare him dead in the eye, whispering my demand. "You'd better."

He nods, a hesitant grin pulling at the corners of his mouth.

I won't let him go.

Not ever again.

II

RHYS

THE BEST THING I'VE FELT IN MY LIFETIME IS WAKING UP TO Aurelia's soft, warm, naked body half on top of me. Her head is resting on my chest, one hand pressing against the scars on my stomach, and one leg curled around mine. Even in sleep, she keeps trying to heal the wounds I've suffered. One of my arms is banded around her back, and the other is buried in her inky-black hair, massaging her scalp.

My mind is drifting, and for once in my life, I'm not focused on anything but the girl in my arms and the next time I can get her to moan for me.

Fates, her sexy, sweet moan.

I want to bottle it—brand it into my brain. I want to

get her to make it a thousand—no, a million—more times. I want to watch her come apart forever. A smile pulls at my lips, and I tug on the sheet covering her luscious ass.

Her body is corded in muscle, but she's soft in all the right places, her beautiful backside being one of them. Carefully rolling us, I get her on her back without rousing her, and then begin my wake-up call with a soft nip at her throat. That earns me a sleepy snuffle, so I move lower and cup her breast with my palm, giving her nipple a gentle tug with my teeth before sucking it into my mouth.

That wins me a squirm. I smile around her breast and move lower.

When I kiss and nip at her ribs and stomach, she gasps awake on a moan. I never knew that was an erogenous zone. Guess you learn something new every day.

"Morning," she grumbles on a husky sigh.

Her lips are swollen from kissing me all night, and she has the epitome of sex hair, but she's never looked more beautiful. Her eyes are half-closed, and that makes me want to do naughty things to fully wake her up.

Maybe when she's slippery and soapy.

"Oh, good. You're awake," I say brightly as if I didn't

just rouse her from a dead sleep. "Wanna take a shower? You're awfully sticky."

One lone eyebrow rises. I have a feeling I'm not going to get much further without some incentive.

"If you get out of bed right now and let me do naughty things to you in the shower, I'll make you an entire pot of coffee."

Her eyes narrow.

Hmm. I'll need more than that. "And I'll make you breakfast."

Her eyes taper into slits.

Not enough, I see. Then I pull out the big guns. "That includes bacon."

"Deal," she says, popping out of bed like a cork.

I've been had. This sexy little minx just played me, and I have *zero* problems with that.

She saunters into the bathroom, naked, like she just won a prize, and if my shitty-ass cooking can be called a trophy, I'm not going to dissuade her. She's brushing her teeth at her vanity, which might be a good idea if I plan on tasting her mouth in the shower. Flipping on the taps of my sink, I watch her spit toothpaste into the basin, but she has her hand blocking her mouth so I can't see her.

It's so cute I have to give her shit for it.

"You're such a girl." I laugh around my toothbrush, foam coating my lips.

"I *am* a girl. And excuse me, but I've never brushed my teeth in front of anyone before. I was trying to be polite. I could be totally gross and hock a huge loogie in front of you—would you like that better?"

Gross. "No. You go right on ahead being girly. I'll be over here not giving you an ounce of shit for it."

With a prim nod, she flounces to the shower like she doesn't have a care in the world. The change in her is remarkable. Yesterday, if someone told me I would see Aurelia flounce *anywhere*, I'd call them a fucking liar.

She warms up the water as I finish up, the sexy silhouette of her curves barely obscured by the fogged glass. I pivot to study her movements as she puts on a little show for me. Meeting my gaze through the shower door, she squeezes soap into her palm and then rubs the suds down her breasts, over her taut, flat stomach and down her smooth thighs. I have to reach behind me to grip the counter, or I'm going to *Hulk*-out and break something. My dick is already standing at full attention.

Quickly, she grants me a reprieve, crooking her finger, and I'm in the shower before she can blink. I step in and turn her body so her back is to me, her smooth, wet skin against mine. My hands take over for hers, and

I run my fingers over the dips and curves of her flesh. I start at her slim neck, running my hands down her shoulders, over the swell of her breasts, watching over her shoulder as her nipples tighten into sharp peaks. She shudders as I circle her ribs with my palms, before I trail feather-light touches down her stomach and between her legs.

She moans when the pad of my thumb finds her clit, getting louder when two fingers tease her opening. Aurelia's squirming now, having the hardest time standing still, and her ass rubs teasingly against my cock. At the brush of skin against skin, my control breaks. I spin her, yanking her up by her ass cheeks and slamming us against the rough tile wall.

Her lips are on mine, her fingers in my hair, and all I can think of is lining my dick up with her wet heat. The soap that only seconds ago was so sexy slipping over her skin is now a serious hindrance.

Finally, I think *fuck it*, and we tumble out of the shower onto the plush bath rug, clawing and tugging at each other in the best kind of frenzy. I sit her squirmy ass on the cold granite vanity, palm my cock, and thrust into her searing, wet heat.

The half-growl, half-moan I get in response goes straight down my spine to my dick. Banding my arm around her back, I grasp her hip with my other hand and start thrusting hard and fast. Her legs wrap around me tight, her heels digging into my ass. Her fingers pull at my hair as her lips suck at my tongue. I'm not going to last, but dammit, she's going to come before me.

Maneuvering my hand between us, I circle her clit with my thumb. I rub once, twice, and then...

"*Rhys*," she gasps, her pussy clamping around my cock like a vise as she comes.

Thank the Fates.

Picking her up off the vanity, we drop to the bath rug. Then I'm driving into her—harder, faster—listening to her moan, her core trembling with aftershocks.

"Baby," she moans, the blissful sound reverberating through my chest.

She's going to come on my cock again. I slam into her, and as her whole body convulses in another orgasm, I lose myself. Thrusting in once more, I plant my shaft, growling into the skin of her neck.

It takes a while to come down, and I struggle to catch my breath, my smugness rising as she tries to do the same.

"Does that still count as naughty things in the shower?" she wheezes. "'Cause I'm hungry, and you promised breakfast."

Nuzzling her breast, I consider teasing her by dragging out the word, "May-be."

And then we get to the hard part—the part I wanted to put off but don't think I can anymore. This is the make-or-break part, and I really hope she's not going to break me.

"You gonna let me kiss you where people can see?"

She seems to ponder the question for a moment. "Probably," she offers with a half-shrug and a sardonic smile. "If you're good and don't piss me off."

She can say what she wants, but I know she means it.

"You gonna stick with me?" I ask as I stare into her mint-green eyes, gauging her expression. "Be with me for real?"

"Yeah, but I think I'm getting the better end of the deal. You just asked a PTSD-having, batshit-crazy seer to be your girl. I think we need to investigate your sanity a teensy bit."

"There is nothing wrong with you," I tell her, brushing a wayward strand of hair from her face. "You are strong and beautiful, and I'm lucky to have you. I just need to buy stock in fire extinguishers. No big."

"Whatever," she mutters, smiling. "Feed me, Handsome."

Then I pull us both up, and she tugs me into the

shower to clean up. We barely make it out of the shower without mauling each other, before throwing on clothes, and heading downstairs to the kitchen hand in hand.

Evan is sitting at the counter shoveling eggs into her mouth fast enough to choke. She nearly does a double take when she sees Aurelia's relaxed shoulders and smile. In all the years I've been around my woman, this is the happiest I've ever seen her. And I've only seen the better parts.

Evan has seen the worst. Or the whatever worst Aurelia would let anyone see.

"You all right there?" she asks Evan, her eyes still wide as she takes Aurelia in.

"Yeah," Evan croaks. "I'm great."

"Is there any more food? I've been promised breakfast, but I'm a little leery of this one's cooking skills."

"Yeah, sure. The eggs should still be warm on the stove, and the bacon is on the counter." She goes to the cabinet, retrieving two plates from the shelf.

"Coffee?" Aurelia asks hopefully as she fills two plates with eggs and bacon.

"Negative, darling. But you have a big strapping man there." Evan winks, smacking me on the shoulder. "Put him to work."

"Yes, I do," she says, shifting to face me. "As per the

terms of our agreement, I am cashing in on that full pot of coffee."

"Done, Gorgeous," I say, trying to make sense of the high-tech gadget masquerading as a coffee pot.

Suddenly, Aurelia gasps, the plates slipping from her fingers, splattering eggs all over the floor. Her eyes flash wide, glowing with white light, her body rigid and bowed in pain. An agonized whimper breaks from her lips. I start for her, but before my fingers can even graze hers, Evan tackles me to the hardwood floor.

"Don't *touch* her," she shouts in my face. "Can't you see it? Her Aegis will *kill* you."

I've never seen an adult Aegis. All the young ones I've known died before they reached maturity. And then the dominos fall in my head, piecing the last century and a half together. I've known about Aurelia's little electricity spurts, the shielding she can create—usually by accident. But Evan has kept the level of her abilities secret from me.

A true Aegis—from what I've read—is outside the Primary's control, having autonomy from visions. They're supposed to be our leaders because they are not ruled by their scant glimpses of fate, not ruled by death.

But none of them have ever survived. I have my suspicions as to why.

No wonder. No fucking wonder why she's been

running. Iva wanted her, and she's been running, hiding this long to remain free. To remain alive.

"Aegis? She's an Aegis, and you didn't think I needed to know?" I roar. "Why the fuck would you keep this from me?"

"Because I told her not to," John calls from the doorway.

I look up from my spot on the floor, noticing the king standing with a vaguely familiar redhead, while simultaneously trying not to throw Evan through a fucking wall. I need to get to Aurelia, and she's in my way.

"And why's that, John?" I grind out through clenched teeth. "What reason could you *possibly have* for not telling me my mate is a fucking time bomb?"

"Because the Primary would have seen," the redhead utters in a soft melodious voice.

"And who the fuck are you?" I ask angrily as I pick myself up off the floor, my eyes assessing every person in the room, but not landing on anyone in particular.

"Oh, don't tell me you don't remember me, child?"

Then I really look at her: the red hair, the blue, sightless eyes. But it's her faint British accent that causes all the memories to come flooding back.

Nicola, the Primary's second.

"You," I growl, lunging viciously at the woman who conned me into binding Aurelia against her will.

I nearly reach her when I'm struck in the temple by a huge hand. It takes a second for the room to swim into focus again, but when it does, Kyle is in between me and my target, looking like the boogeyman from a nightmare.

What the actual fuck?

His black hair is disheveled, eyes full black, and his thick fingers have curled into talons. Hissing at me through two-inch fangs, the hulking man is standing between Nicola and I, his arms thrown wide to prevent me from getting to her.

Why is he protecting her? Other than Aurelia and me, I've never seen a wraith give two shits about a phoenix in my life, and vice versa.

I'm two seconds away from pulling my Ruger and putting a bullet in his head when Nicola intervenes. She gently places her dainty hand on his shoulder, instantly calming him. His sclera bleeds back to white, and his hands uncurl, the talons retracting into his nail beds. His fangs are the last to go, the dull crunch of bone reforming in his jaw causing my stomach to turn.

I make the mistake of relaxing my posture, and then like the fucking asshole he is, he strikes, tackling me to the ground with his forearm against my neck. Before I can retaliate in kind, Aurelia gasps.

Then she screams.

She screams so loud and so long, I know I'm going to kill whatever monster is haunting her.

No matter what.

12

AURELIA

THE POWER IS OUT, DARKNESS SURROUNDS ME. THE QUICK pained breaths of the injured fills my ears. Lightning slashes across the sky outside, swiftly followed by the roar of thunder. In the scant glimpse of light, puddles of blood and water from the sprinkler system appear, pooling on the hardwood floor of the great room. The broken ruins of lamps are strewn across the wood, alongside jagged shards of the largest window.

The safe house wasn't so safe after all.

My feet are bare, the hem of my already-sodden jeans sucking up the watered-down blood from the floor. The shush of feet moving through the water reaches me, quiet as the flutter of a butterfly's wing. In the darkness, I can't tell if the person is friend or foe. My gut goes with foe, and I tighten my grip on the butcher knife in my hand, ready for anything.

I've been searching for Rhys for what seems like hours, but I know it's only been mere minutes since the siege began on the house. Either Rhys has left me to stave off this attack alone, or he's keeping someone else safe.

Either way, he's not with me.

We got separated, and I can't remember the reason, but now I can't find him anywhere in this pitch-black Hell. I remember reading once that Hell was as black as a moonless night, and they—whoever they were—are right. I'm tortured more by fear of the unknown and what I can't see than I am by anything else that has transpired here.

Clearing the great room and the kitchen, I check the pulses of a lifeless Cam and Asher as I go. Judging by the open maw that used to be Asher's neck, he died quickly. Cam's death was slower—his intestines spilled from his belly onto the kitchen floor. But with each person I find—every single one—has lost their life.

I fear that everyone is dead.

I can't find Evan, West, John, or any of the other guards who were here with us. I can't find anyone alive in this blackness. I fear if I set myself aglow, using myself for light, it will give away my location. My shield is pointless as well, since the house is flooded in an inch of water. It would elec-

trocute anyone touching the ground. Maybe they wouldn't die a true death, but in this pit, I fear hurting someone.

What good are powers if you can't use them?

A hard hand grips my hair—the braid used as a handle as my neck is stretched backward. The thick, cold bite of a knife is thrust against my skin, nearly nicking the flesh. My worry of being found is gone, and my whole body ignites, fire racing over my skin, burning whoever's holding me. The pained growl of a man sounds loud in the dim as I'm released.

A phoenix wouldn't be burned by my flames—only a wraith would.

I turn to see Carver's naturally bronze skin red and puckered from the flames, rapidly healing from the burn. He smiles, his hard lips pulling into a cruel smirk, as he removes a blade from his belt, his other hand holding an intricately crafted short sword. The betrayal burns in my chest. I knew we had a traitor in our midst, but I thought better of Carver.

I thought he was a friend.

"Why?" I plead. "Why would you kill your friends? Why would you do this?"

"I didn't kill them. You did," he hisses. "Just by being here, you damned us all. I'm only trying to live. If I give you over, I'll keep breathing, and breathing is my top priority. Your safety and the ideals of your ridiculous war are not."

His eyes flick just to the left of my head and then back to me.

Before I can move, he has disappeared like smoke, reappearing at my left. I step to counter, but I'm not fast enough. The dagger slides between my ribs, stabbing my lung, cutting off my pained cry.

"Quiet, my beauty," he whispers into my ear, his lips soft on my skin. "I will keep him safe for you until we get you out of there." He slows my crumpling body before it can hit the floor, my flames extinguishing as my light goes out.

I SUCK IN A HUGE BREATH AS I EMERGE FROM THE VISION, BUT only in preparation for the scream clawing its way up my throat. It takes a second, but it finally breaks through the barrier of my teeth. My shield comes up hard enough that it cracks the stone island I'm clinging to, the hiss of the stone cleaving into pieces rattling through my chest.

My sight hasn't returned yet, and I don't know where Rhys is. My fingers reluctantly release the rubble of the countertop as I reach out into the darkness to find him.

"Rhys," I shriek, grasping at nothing. "We have to

go. We have to go right now. *Rhys*. Where are you? *We have to go right now.*"

Fates, it's never taken so long to get my sight back after a vision. Even after the bad ones, it's usually only taken a few moments.

Where is he? We have to get out of here before they come. Stumbling a little, I plop gracelessly onto the hardwood floor.

The shuffling of feet and the thud of something large—maybe a person—hit the ground, quickly followed by a mumbled curse. *Definitely a person.* And by that curse, I'm going with it being Kyle.

"Baby, I'm here," Rhys murmurs, his hands cupping my face as he smears the wetness there.

"Your eyes are bleeding, baby," he says in gruff concern, his voice low enough to be classified as a whisper.

I realize now that there are many people in this room. I knew Evan was here, but now I sense the signatures of several people—possibly the whole house—are here with us.

"I don't care. We have to go right now," I repeat on a hiss. "Get my keys and go-bag and anything you need. We have to leave this house."

Blinking, the blackness starts to fade as light finally blooms, lifting the pall of blindness. When my eyes focus on his face, he clutches me to him, turning us, so his back is to the gathering crowd.

"Whatever you saw, can it wait a few hours?" he mutters into my hair. "We have a huge fucking problem."

His fingers massage my scalp, trying to calm me I suspect, but even his touch isn't helping right now.

He didn't see.

"I don't know. I know once the rain starts it'll be too late. Soldiers are coming, and people will die here. I was wearing this outfit, meaning it happens today. We. Have. To. Leave. Do you understand? They are coming for us."

"I know," he assures me, "but I need you to stay calm and hang in there a little while longer. We have a hiccup we need to iron out before we go."

Bracing myself for whatever has Rhys in such a twist, I spot a flash of red hair that makes me freeze. Standing behind the protective trunk of Kyle's arm is a bitch I hoped I'd never see again. Before he knows what hit him, I've forced Rhys behind me, my arm thrown back to prevent him from going forward, enveloping us in my shield.

That's new. Didn't know I could do that.

"John. What in the hell is that bitch doing here?" I

snarl, my voice distorted from speaking through clenched teeth.

Yeah, I'm steadfastly ignoring the fact I'm doing something that should be impossible.

"I'm only here to help you," Nicola insists, her blind ice-blue eyes trying to meet mine but missing the mark.

She's the only oracle with her eyes still intact since she was born blind. Because of that defect, her visions have been "pure" since birth. She is the only oracle with zero bonds to Iva and probably the only one able to usurp her.

But did that little bitch help me?

No. She didn't.

She betrayed me instead.

"And I should believe that why, exactly?" I growl. "I remember how much your 'help' worked last time."

Nicola sighs, pinching the bridge of her nose like she's trying to gather the patience to talk to a toddler. "I merely told you the rules of the covenant—you chose to do what you wished. I cannot control the actions of the people around me. And I cannot foresee *every* action by *every* person. I'm not omnipotent, and I'm not infallible. And I tried to right my wrong. Who do you think pulled the soldiers from your cell so he could get you out, *hmm*? If you think he did that one on his own, you're sadly mistaken." She nods in the general direction of Rhys.

"You told me my daughter would be beautiful," I croak, tears clogging my throat. "That even though she would have my eyes, she would grow up outside the Legion, never to be mired in the chains of the Primary. You told me she would live. You *lied*."

It kills me to know that I'm more torn up about the baby I lost than the husband I took to the funeral pyre. I had Lucien longer—I knew him, loved him. But the more I think of how much I missed not seeing my child come into the world—not seeing her smile, not hearing her laugh—the more I hate Nicola for giving me that hope.

In my gut, I knew we weren't going to make it— knew something bad was going to happen. I just assumed it would be a complicated birth, not that I wouldn't even get to have her at all.

Or any child for that matter.

"You may think what you wish, but I did not lie," she snarls, her eyes flashing a brilliant blue. "I'm here to help. And you will sit there. And. Let. Me. Speak."

It takes everything I have—every single ounce of restraint I possess—to not jump over the ruined kitchen island and punch her right in the fucking face. The nerve of this bitch.

"*I did not lie.*"

My ass.

Considering I can't have any more children—hell yes, she fucking well lied. I give her a look of death she can't see and mutter, "Fine," under my breath.

I drop my shield, and Kyle's posture immediately relaxes. If I didn't know better, I'd think the brute of a wraith wanted into the Ice Queen's pants.

Good luck there, pal.

Wraiths have some severe mating habits. While phoenixes are a matriarchal society, wraiths are predominantly run by the males. I figure it's mostly due to the wraith male's irrational need to protect their mate. If Kyle thinks Nicola is his mate, there is no order he will follow, no rule he won't break for her. If that's what is going on here, Nicola just bought herself a six-foot-seven burly-as-fuck shadow.

"I have reason to believe that your visions have been infiltrated by Iva. From what I understand, she is sending them to you—ones you can't change or interpret until the event has come to pass or is too close to be prevented. It's punishment for you both, but more for you, Rhys."

"Why is she punishing Rhys?" I ask, confused. "Because he didn't want to be my soldier? Because that's cracked, even for her crazy ass."

"Oh, child," Nicola tsks. "You don't know?" She tilts her head in Rhys' direction, but her eyes miss the mark again, drifting toward the light of the picture window behind us. "Why haven't you told her?"

"Because I didn't want her to hate me more than she already did, maybe?" Rhys says scathingly. "You've already let the cat out of the bag—might as well tell her the rest. I've had her to myself for less than twenty-four hours, but you go right on ahead and ruin it."

An expression of disapproval flashes across her face, and Nicola's lips screw into a grimace.

"Anyone want to tell me what the fuck is going on?" I gripe, tossing up my hands.

"She is punishing Rhys for betraying the Legion," Nicola confesses. "Rhys' brother, Julian, was to assassinate Olivia Black before the conception of her next child. It was to look like a rival's kill and not lead back to the Legion. Julian told Rhys of his assignment and refused to be dissuaded from his task. In turn, Rhys delivered Julian to the wraiths to prevent Olivia's murder."

"And because you gave your brother over," I muse, "you saved Olivia, and Evan got to be born? And I'd hate you because of that, why?" I tilt my head slightly to the side to see his expression.

His jaw clenches as he grips the back of his neck,

refusing to look me in the eye. "Because my actions resulted in us being bound against your consent as punishment? Because I chose a stranger over my own brother? Really? Take your pick."

"So, you think I'm such a heartless cow that I'd approve of the murder of a harmless woman to prevent my own suffering?" I ask incredulously.

"I don't think you're a heartless cow," he murmurs, finally meeting my gaze. "I just thought you wouldn't see my side."

"Even when I hated you, I still saw your side. I'm not going to fault you for things you did to save someone else. That's just not in me."

"I just didn't want you to hate me anymore."

"I won't. Can we discuss this shit another time? Say, when we aren't in a serious time crunch of impending death? Because I gotta say, this 'We're Gonna Die' bullshit is getting old."

Rhys inclines his head in agreement and shifts to face Nicola. "So, are soldiers really coming, or has Iva cracked the lock on Aurelia's head for real?"

Nicola seems to think about it for a moment. "I believe she's still having trouble due to Aurelia being Aegis. Aurelia's visions of herself seem to be on the level, it's just the visions outside herself that appear to be affected. If you tell me what you saw, I could tell you if it is from Iva or from beyond the veil."

"Whoa, whoa, whoa," I bark. "Who said anything about an Aegis? *Who* the fuck is an Aegis? I know it's not me because all the Aegis I know died before maturity because they fucking vaporized themselves, and whatever way they did it, they didn't come back."

I'm half-shouting at Nicola now because the border of ridiculous has just been crossed.

"And what would a power-hungry diabolical bitch of a leader do if she found one that could survive into maturity?" Evan pipes up from the circle of West's arms. "She'd either bind you as an oracle so she could control what you see—or kill you. Since she can't do one, she's damn well going to try the other."

I pinch my brow, my brain on fire. "And by getting into my head she accomplishes *what*?"

"She gets to torture you—make you crazy. She gets to change that strong-willed, beautiful girl I fell in love with into a freaking hermit," Rhys answers, his voice ravaged. "She gets to twist the knife in my gut because I'm the reason she's doing this."

"But if I'm an Aegis—not that I believe you— wouldn't she have come after me, anyway?"

"It is possible," Nicola murmurs with a slight tilt of her head, "but unlikely. Your full potential was not known to us when you left. Or more accurately, I didn't inform Iva of the full scope of your potential. By that time, I had begun to make moves to remove oracles from her numbers."

"Well, aren't you a fucking saint," I snap sarcastically.

"You know, child, I am supremely fed up with your cheek. May I remind you, I am your elder, your Secondary, and your bloody savior. Show me some respect, or I will let your impertinent hide swing in the wind."

"Look, lady. I don't owe you a fucking thing. The way I see it, either Iva wants something from me, or you do. I'm not sure what it is yet, but I gotta tell ya, I'm disinclined to give it to you. Now you can take that savior shit and shove it right next to the stick rammed up your ass."

"Aurelia, dear," John tries to interject, "let's not piss off the only person who can save our collective asses?"

"She's not going to save shit." I scoff, my lip curled into a sneer. "Look, I'm sorry if this screws with your plan, but I'm not about to make a deal with the devil and get fuck-all in return. I'm leaving, and I'm taking Rhys with me. Anyone else staying, I suggest you get ready because soldiers are coming, and as far as I can see, no one but Carver makes it."

Carver's arm is thrown over his husband's shoulder, holding the smaller man in a loose embrace. Javier appears worried, and if the darkening of his eyes is any indication, he's about two steps away from phasing.

"Oh, and Carver?" His eyes cut to me, furious and worried and blackening into an almost-full phase.

"Yes, ma'am?" he hisses through lengthening fangs.

"If you have some grand plan to hand me over to the enemy to save you and your husband's asses?" I lift a brow in challenge. "Don't."

13

RHYS

I'm going to ruin everything.

I don't want to, but I have to stop my woman from doing something stupid out of spite.

Aurelia is furiously packing, shoving articles of clothing and toiletries into her bag with enough force to split the seams of the duffle. She's quick and efficient, and if I don't hurry, she'll be out the door before I can stop her.

As much as it hurts me to admit, we have to hear Nicola out.

"Gorgeous," I call, but she doesn't stop moving—she doesn't even look at me.

She takes a thick stack of bills and throws it in the duffle, and then gathers up the next.

"Aurelia, stop," I murmur, catching her hand as she passes, reeling her into the space between my knees.

My fingers span her denim-clad hips, and I peer into her beautiful pale eyes. Worry and anger wrench her features and I reach up, cupping her jaw, bringing her face to mine. She tries to give me a quick peck, but my tongue sweeps the line of her lips. She opens her mouth, giving me a begrudging moan in response.

Leaning back, I pull her on top of me as I quickly flip us, resting my weight on my forearms between the legs of my reluctant beauty. In a lust-filled haze, I sadly part from her lips, pressing my forehead against hers for a moment before pulling my face away. I've got to get my dick under control, or I'll forget what I was going to say.

"We have to talk before we do something we can't take back," I gently appeal, praying she'll listen to me for once. "I think we need to hear Nicola out. We at least need to find out if she knows whether soldiers are really coming or not. We owe it to them."

"Because you think my visions are unreliable?" she croaks with a rueful twist to her mouth.

"Given what we know now," I murmur as I massage her scalp, "I don't think we can trust them one hundred percent."

"You're probably right," she grumbles, "but it kills me to give that cow the satisfaction."

"I agree, but it's the right thing to do."

"Um-kay," she grouses. "How do you suggest we go about it?"

"I think she's telling the truth about the Aegis. I've seen you. You use an electrified shield, darling. Just because you can't always control it, doesn't mean it's not there. And who's to say that the others wouldn't have lived? I don't put it past Iva to exterminate an entire faction of phoenixes to secure her throne. Do you?"

"No," she admits. "I wouldn't put it past her. How many of those children did she kill?"

"If I'm going with my gut?" The enormity of it all turns my stomach. "All of them."

Fucking genocide.

"*Fates.* How long has she been Primary?" she asks, pressing against my chest and sitting up. "Has she been killing Aegis children this *whole* time? Why hasn't anyone noticed or done anything about it?"

Aurelia gulps back tears, pressing a hand over her heart. "Then she's killed them her entire reign."

"Yeah."

"She's been Primary for the last six hundred years," she breathes, realization dawning on her face. "There have been at least two Aegis deaths a year—sometimes more—so at the bare minimum, twelve hundred children have died. She's a fucking mass murderer."

"So instead of running from this bitch, we should probably fight."

"Probably?" She shoots me a searing glare. "Ya think?"

"Okay, more than probably," I concede. "Definitely. This has gone on too long."

"That, we can agree on," she says, pacing the length of the room. "But I refuse to be nice to that lying sack of shit."

Fair enough.

A knock comes at the door, but before I can open it, Carver pops into our room in a swath of black smoke. I'm positive the expression on my face tells him this intrusion is *not* welcome.

"What?" Carver shrugs. "I knocked first."

"What are you doing here?" Aurelia asks, her hands crackling with electricity.

I'm a little afraid she's going to kill first and worry about the consequences later.

"I need to know what you saw," Carver demands irritably.

"Why?" Aurelia growls. "So you can stab me in the chest sooner? No thanks, dick."

"Look," he placates, holding up his hands in surrender, "I don't know what you saw, but I wouldn't do something like that."

"Sure you wouldn't," Aurelia agrees sarcastically as her eyes begin to glow. "You wouldn't lie to me either, now, would you?"

"Dammit. Am I going to be judged for trying to keep the fucking peace? *Fine*. Yes, I lied when I said I forgot why Asher and Cam were fighting. I wanted you to feel safe here, and I didn't want you to hate Cam, okay?" Carver tosses his hands to the side in frustration. "Cam is a good guy—he's just a little pissed right now. He has family in Cortez, or he *had* family in Cortez. He lost contact with them about a week ago, and when he went to check on them, he found the whole place burned to the fucking ground. Cam doesn't want you here. He doesn't want Iva here. He sure as shit doesn't want any more war. He was rather vocal about it, and Asher shut him down."

"You're right," Aurelia admits. "I wouldn't have felt safe here, and for good reason."

"And there's no way we would have stayed." I interject, finishing Aurelia's thought. "Is there some reason *you* want us here, Carver?"

"Yes, there's a reason. In case you haven't realized this yet, Iva is having us exterminated like we're motherfucking roaches. Like our truce means nothing. And I know what you phoenixes think of us, okay? Most of you believe wraiths are worse than dog shit on the bottom of your boot, but dammit, we're people, too. And we serve a purpose. It might be awful, but it is necessary, and I'm not going to be ashamed of how I was born."

Wraiths are the trash collectors of the supernatural community. They ferry deceased evil souls to Hell—Ethereal and human alike. To do that, they must consume them. It's a nasty process that no one wants to witness—or be a part of—for that matter.

Phoenixes, in turn, are supposed to ferry all other souls to be reborn. There is obviously a rift between the two species when there shouldn't be. Why people give a shit who does what, I can't fathom, but it's common for phoenixes to be snooty elitists with sticks up their asses.

"What the fuck do you mean, 'you phoenixes'?" Aurelia squawks incredulously. "My best friend in the whole world is a wraith. I understand your purpose, and I commend you for it. I couldn't do what you do—consuming that much evil without going crazy. I can't possibly imagine what you must go through to do that job."

"So *not* the point," Carver says, punctuating each

word with a clap of his hands. "I want to know what you saw."

"Come with us to talk to Nicola," Aurelia offers. "I'll tell you both at the same time."

"Fine," he agrees and smokes out.

"Why do they do that? It's not that far of a walk." The whole "poofing" thing is fucking annoying.

I grab Aurelia's duffel, and we head down the hallway to the bottom-level game room. John is sitting in his comfortable leather armchair, half-sprawled, with his head in his hands. He seems to be either trying to rip his hair out or squish his own skull.

Cam and Asher are on either side of his chair, standing like sentries. Nicola is perched on his right with a glass of iced tea in her hand. She appears at ease, either because she knew we were coming, or because she has little to fear with Kyle at her side. Kyle is smugly lounging on the couch next to Nicola with his arm thrown over the back near her shoulders.

I make a mental note to kick his ass in the near future.

Aidan and Ian are sitting at the bar, looking worried and spoiling for a fight. Evan and West are sitting on the loveseat next to the pool table. Evan has her hand entwined with West's, squeezing it hard enough I can hear his bones creaking from here.

"Come to ask me for forgiveness?" Nicola asks, and I suppress a growl.

"Fuck, no," Aurelia answers just as Carver emerges from the hidden basement door. "I came to ask you if Iva's been killing the Aegis her entire reign. I also want to know if soldiers are coming tonight during a thunderstorm. And finally, I want to know if old Carver here is going to get the chance to stab me in the fucking lung."

Javier is on his husband's heels and goes from a smiley, good-natured guy to half-phased in less than a second. "Carver wouldn't do something like that."

"Yes, he would," Nicola counters. "If it meant that you would live, he would do anything. You know that." Her eyes drift in our direction. "I am—what's the word you used earlier? Oh, yes. I am disinclined to answer your questions."

"Look, you catty little bitch," Aurelia says with a cruel twist of her mouth. "I've had about enough. I didn't like you one hundred and sixty years ago, and I sure as shit don't like you now. But it's good you're showing your true colors in front of the people who could be killed if you hesitate. I love how you are so reluctant to stop mass murder. I love how fucking cruel you're being right now. Because you can't see the look on their faces, but I can, and it's just dawning on them that you're no better than Iva. You're just wrapped in a different fucking package."

"Do. Not. Compare me to that bloody woman," Nicola snarls, abruptly rising to her feet, the glass in her hand shattering from the force of her grip.

"Then don't act like her," I growl. "What's your problem? You came to us. Just talk to us without the ridiculous hierarchy you've made up in your head. We're not going to bow to you. Get over it."

"Right. Just answer your questions, because that's all I'm bloody well good for. Absolutely," Nicola says bitterly. "I don't know if Iva has killed the Aegis children. She has shielded herself from my abilities, more so over the last year. She is an expert at hiding herself. Based on the atrocities she has committed over the last three centuries I have been with her, it is within her character. I don't know if soldiers are coming here today. My future is unclear to me and has been for the last three weeks. I can see other peoples near future, but the past few days..." She trails off, shaking her head before lowering herself onto the couch. "I don't know. And yes, Carver would stab his best friend in the back to save his husband. But you all knew that already."

"Great," Aurelia quips. "You know exactly dick. Awesome."

"Oh, I know a few things," Nicola insists, her tone

ominous. "Your future just isn't one of them. I know Iva is sending soldiers away from their charges to exterminate wraiths, leaving their oracles unprotected. I know she has sequestered the scholars away from their families. I know the oracle population has grown over thirty percent in the last century, and their numbers have increased to the highest our race has ever had. I know she has revoked the exile covenant, and any seer who refuses the transition to oracle is put to death. And the gentry have been called back from their posts. They are no longer sending souls on to be reborn. As I said, I know plenty. I just don't know what happens today."

"Are the head families just letting this happen?" I whisper in utter disbelief.

"Yes. All four of the original families have several oracles under Iva's care," Nicola answers matter-of-factly. "She can do whatever she wants, and their soldiers are not there to protect them."

"Well, fuck. So, we can't leave, and we have to stop the bitch." I direct my attention to the king. "John, how do you want to play this?"

"We have plenty of weapons in the house, and there is a bunker hidden under the basement gym. Those who cannot fight should be taken to safety," John says, likely referring to Nicola and Evan, even though Evan can hold her own.

"John, I think you should leave," Aurelia cautions. "I saw Asher and Cam ripped to shreds in my vision. Can they go as your guard? I don't know who wants to stay, but those two need to get out of here."

"I must go as well. But I won't go far," Nicola says, her face almost appearing sheepish at the confession of her inability. "Without my visions, I am of little use in combat."

"I'll go with you," Kyle says gruffly.

Nicola's head tilts toward the sound of his voice, and she reluctantly nods.

"Okay, who's staying?" I ask as a roaring clap of thunder shakes the house, and the lights flicker out.

"Everyone," Aurelia whispers. "It's too late."

14

AURELIA

"Can you get her out of here?" I ask Kyle, jerking my chin in Nicola's direction.

"Absolutely," he says as he grabs her up from the couch, surrounding her with his thick arms. "I'll be back as soon as she's safe." He promptly smokes out of the room, leaving faint whisps of blackness in his wake.

Now that I think about it, all the wraiths could abandon us here to die—just up and leave us to Iva's little invasion. The dread growing in my stomach swells so big, I think I'll drown in it. I shift my gaze to Evan, and it's as if she can read my mind. She shakes her head at me.

She won't leave us.

No matter what.

That assurance has a gust of a sigh wheezing from my lips, my anxiety cooling for a second.

Rhys has already drawn his Ruger, his eyes scanning the room for threats. He has positioned his body so he's between me and the glass French doors leading to the bottom deck. A slight hint of ambient light filters through the glass, but it's quickly fading as the storm gathers strength.

"We need weapons," Evan whispers. "Lots and lots of weapons. I'm going downstairs. Papa, I want you with me."

John appears reluctant. Moreover, he seems kind of off. For the first time, I notice the dark circles under his eyes, disheveled hair, and his haggard expression lined with fatigue. Come to think of it, no one has mentioned his wife, Olivia.

We've been here two days, and I haven't seen her once. Bonded wraiths aren't frequently without their other half—the tie to their spouse soul-deep. Suddenly, I realize that I haven't seen Olivia in months. I've talked to Evan about her in passing, but I haven't clapped eyes on her. Even when I sparred with John at their house, I didn't see her.

Have I been such a selfish asshole that I didn't notice?

Yes. Yes, I have.

The pit in my stomach turns into a boulder, and it's hard to keep the shame off my face. I'm an awful friend.

West is hovering at Evan's left and appears as if he's two seconds away from dragging her to the sub-basement bunker and chaining her there. Finally, he breaks and interrupts the father-daughter stare down that's been going on for some time. Grabbing Evan by the waist, he hauls her to the open basement stairwell.

John, Cam, and Asher follow. Cam and Asher are bringing up the rear, both with their guns drawn. I can't see the make or model in the dim, but I do recognize the suppressors attached to the barrels of their handguns. This makes me feel better. Using firearms in this enclosed space will fuck with our hearing. The suppressors will at least lessen that blow. Even so, I'm pretty sure I'm sticking with silent killers.

Evan pops back into the room. In a rush, she shoves a pile of weapons and holsters at me. I inspect the haul and have to hold in my squeal of delight.

So not appropriate.

"Thank you," I whisper as I yank her into a quick hug.

I start arranging my weapons as she pops back out —first by putting my braided hair in a bun with the handful of throwing spikes as hair sticks. Then I swing a back holster over my shoulders, a lovely pair of hatchets fitting in the leather perfectly. Strapping a bandolier filled with throwing knives on my right thigh, I make sure to seat each one. All that's left is to chamber a round in the small Glock 19 before stuffing the extra mags in my pockets.

Evan knows me so well. If we survive this, I'll need to send her a fruit basket or something.

My spritely friend pops back in the room with West begrudgingly in tow. He helps outfit Aidan, Ian, and Rhys with bladed weapons. Carver and Javier have drifted closer to the mouth of the staircase leading to the upper levels, quietly arguing in Portuguese.

But I don't have time to worry about their little spat. Knowledge filters into my brain, and now I'm certain the vision I had in the kitchen is absolutely correct. Twenty or so men are outside, moving through the trees toward the house. They haven't even set off an alarm yet, but I have no doubt in my mind they're out there.

I really, really hate being right.

"I don't give a fuck what Nicola says," I hiss, meeting Evan's gaze. "My visions have always been spot on. Not a single one hasn't come true, but I've never had this much warning before. So, we need a game plan. Now that they've moved in closer, I can sense approximately twenty soldiers out there, but there could be more in another wave."

"That's what you saw?" Carver breathes, pushing back into the room. "No, you're leaving something out. Tell us the rest." He shakes off his husband's hold, barking at him in Portuguese when he tries to pull him back.

"Fine. A brief rundown? They trigger the sprinkler system somehow. I can't find any of you, but I do find Asher with his head almost cut off, and Cam disemboweled." Now I get to the rough part that's going to make Rhys lose his shit. I don't look at him, instead pinning my gaze on the man I'm about to tattle on. "Carver catches me unaware and stabs me in the chest. But he lets me know he's going to keep an eye out for Rhys, and that you guys are going to save me. To date, it is the most changeable, in-advance vision I've ever had."

Just as I expected, a snarl erupts from Rhys' throat, his big body herding me back and away from the group, Carver especially. He chambers a round in threat, his skin flushing with the heat of his Fireskin. If he's not careful, he'll phase right here in the game room.

Carver advances, holding up his hands in surrender, a pleading expression pulling at his brow. "I wouldn't. I won't."

We both know he would if it meant keeping

everyone else safe, and I hate to agree with him. If it meant that everyone else in this room would live, I'd do the same to him. I wouldn't like it, but I would do it.

Especially if it kept Rhys safe.

"We can change it," I whisper to Rhys' taught shoulders. "This one doesn't have to come true."

"Then let's change the motherfucker," Rhys growls, slicing a look at me over his shoulder. "No one goes anywhere alone. We stay in pairs. They are coming to find us—to kill us. Let's remind them what real warriors can do."

"Where are they coming in?" West asks, adjusting his weapons.

My eyes lose focus for a second as I allow the knowledge to filter into my brain. "Second- and third-floor picture windows," I answer, jerking my head upward. "They're repelling from the roof."

"Good luck getting through the glass," Evan mutters with a scoff. "It would take a damn cannon to break it. Why aren't they flying in?"

"Because they plan on leaving with a hostage," West replies, clearly referring to me.

He's not wrong. It's the only thing that makes any sense.

"I want you guys to dispatch any soul you feel is

evil," Rhys demands. "Glut yourselves if you have to. We need to weed out those motherfuckers—quick."

"It would be my pleasure," Aidan agrees with an evil smile even I can see in the dim. He shares a look with Ian, and together, they silently head up the stairs.

Carver and Javier move to the second floor, Rhys and I go to the first, leaving Evan and West to the bottom floor closest to the hidden basement door.

In some ways, it's fortunate the only entry and exit points are all located on the south side of the house. Since the garage takes up the entire northwest section, the only entry points are security-enhanced doors that close like a vaulted safe when the power is cut.

However, the system *does* have a fail-safe. One that only triggers in the event of a fire.

Fuck. Just as I think this, the sprinkler system goes off, the hiss of the automatic locks disengaging, gusting through the house.

Son of a bitch.

"They are using it as a diversion," I breathe to Rhys from our perch on the staircase leading to the first floor. A shiver rattles through me at the freezing water falling in a torrent around us. "Five are on standby to see where the biggest threat is. Three are coming in the third-floor window, five through the second. Seven are now planning to go through the first-floor window in the great room."

I *see* them in my mind. I can feel them like a jagged nail scratching into my brain—their racing heartbeats, their minds buzzing in preparation for the fight, their smug boasting of who can kill the most wraiths.

Bastards.

"Bottom floor?" he asks, the cold not appearing to affect him at all.

My head gives a faint shake without me telling it to. "None yet."

"Well, let's get to it. I'm warning you—you better stay with me," he demands on a whisper. "Don't you dare leave my side."

Swallowing hard, I give him a tremulous shake of my head. "I won't. I'm sticking with you, remember?"

After one hundred and sixty years of loneliness, I finally have something worth living for. Just the thought of losing what we have makes my chest ache.

Rhys studies my face for a moment before hooking a rough hand around the back of my neck, hauling me to him. His breath whispers across my lips, his fear palpable with every single passing second.

"I love you, Gorgeous," he murmurs before dropping a short, fevered kiss to my lips. "Always."

"Always," I repeat, touching my forehead to his.

I'm going to keep us alive. I am.

I have to.

Before we leave our positions, I silently slide off my leather-bottomed sandals, their slick soles more of a hindrance than a help.

Barefoot.

I don't want to be barefoot. It's too close to my vision.

Rhys takes point. He's up the three steps and in the hallway leading to the great room, before the window breaks. The poor bastards trying to break it didn't anticipate reinforced glass, though, and the compact battering ram they're using isn't quite doing the job.

Then an enormous phoenix shoves past the others, the hulking giant easily the biggest Ethereal I've ever seen in my entire life. He appears to consider the glass for a minute, then lifts his boat-sized boot and simply kicks the window in.

I pause to reconsider my weapon choice. I'm not sure a nine-millimeter bullet is going to cut it with this burly bastard, but I'm going to give it the old college try. Waiting for the next crack of thunder to muffle my shot, I take aim for the only spot on his body not covered in body armor.

Three rapid-fire squeezes of my trigger, and he goes down like a stone.

Rhys uses his lifeless body as a springboard and tears into the next soldier with a curved blade resembling a machete. His target's head goes flying as his body falls, and Rhys is on to the next. I don't stop firing, taking out two more phoenixes before my mag runs out. Tossing the spent pistol, I swiftly draw the hatchets from their sheaths, weighing the weapons in my palms before I strike at the last man left standing.

He seems shocked at the sight of his fallen brethren but snaps out of it as I approach. He barely has enough time to raise his weapon before I'm on him, and he has the business end of my blade embedded into his eye.

It's swiftly dawning on me that this has to be the first wave. There is no way it could be this easy to dispatch seven men.

Other than the pattering of the artificial rain, the rest of the house is silent. No shots fired, no creaks of steps on the hardwood floors. Nothing.

The dread in the pit of my stomach doubles in size.

"This doesn't feel right," I whisper to Rhys. "It shouldn't be this easy. We're missing something."

He nods in agreement, signaling for me to follow him.

We head back downstairs to check on Evan and West. Each step feels like a land mine. Rhys, finally tired of the lack of light, ignites his Fireskin in a controlled burn. The flames don't deviate from his palm as he uses his fingers like a torch.

Evan and West are standing out of the way of the French doors, wary of an attack from all angles.

"You guys good?" Rhys asks, his gaze scanning the room for threats.

West nods in response, and Evan appears simultaneously bored and worried out of her mind.

"Tell me this doesn't feel right," Rhys grouses.

"Nope," West grumbles. "This feels like one big con."

"I can't see anything," I admit, frustrated as hell. "I don't know what's going on, but no one is waiting to get in. No one else is out there. Whatever threat there is, it's already inside."

West suggests we move together to find the others, and we head to the second floor in search of Javier and Carver. We find neither, but we do see a mound of bodies.

"*Fates save us,*" Evan exclaims, stumbling back as she covers her mouth.

She can obviously see something I can't, because the

expression of sheer terror in her eyes is enough to chill my blood.

"Revenant," she murmurs, clearly aghast. "Their hearts are missing."

Rhys brings his fist closer to the bodies, the faint flicker of light illuminating the macabre scene. The floor and walls are spattered in scarlet, the lifeless men lying in a heap of blood and gore and bone.

Whatever tore out their organs was strong enough to go through their body armor like tissue paper.

"*What*," I hiss, shaking, "the *fuck* is a Revenant?"

But it's West who answers me. "It's what happens to wraiths when they go crazy. They start eating the flesh of the dead. But I've never seen one eat from the living or even kill to get a meal."

"And how do you kill one?" I ask, my voice growing even smaller, because *holy fucking shit.*

"Fire," he replies, his gaze still locked on the gruesome pile.

Well, yippee. At least we have that.

In pairs, we move on, Evan and West searching the northwest section of the floor and Rhys and I looking in the southeast. Together, we clear our room, our bathroom, and the next guest room, only finding one body with his heart still intact. His head, though, is another story.

We make our way back to the rally point, where Evan and West hover around an unconscious Aidan and a critically injured Ian. West is working on Ian, trying to staunch the flow of blood from his neck with Evan's thin cardigan. Ian's eyes roll in his head, a gurgling gasp rattling from his throat.

He's so close to death, but his future is an unknown. I suppose that's a good thing.

"There are medical supplies in the bunker," Evan says. "If I can get him there and stop the bleeding, he'll survive."

I pray she's right.

"Take him," West orders, and Evan grabs him, disappearing in a whisp of smoke.

"Can he not heal like the rest of you?" I ask before the answer filters into my brain. Ian isn't like his brother.

"No," West answers, his jaw clenched tight. "Ian's different. He can't travel like us or heal as quickly, but he has our lifespan and our purpose. We think maybe his mother was human, but none of us know for sure."

Rhys and I nod in understanding. It has happened with our species as well when they mate with humans. I can understand the appeal, but I have a serious issue with the logistics. There is no way to extend their human's lifespan.

No spell.

No remedy.

Nothing to stave off the human condition.

"What about Aidan?" I ask. "Is he all right?"

"Not sure," West replies with a shake of his head. "Won't be sure until we get him in the med bay."

"His breathing isn't labored, he's not bleeding from anywhere but his head, and that seems to be closing up. Let's find Carver and Javi and then get the fuck out of here," Rhys suggests. "You stay with him, Gorgeous. West and I'll check upstairs real quick. Don't move, got it?"

If it were any other time, I'd do something cute like flip him off, but all I can do is nod. The loft is small enough they won't be gone too long. Readjusting the grip on my hatchets, I scan the landing and hallway for threats as the boys head upstairs.

As good as my ears are, I don't hear him until he's three feet from me. And as good as my sight is, I don't see him at all. The monster of a man takes another step closer, as silent as the grave, the scent of death the only thing heralding his presence.

By the time I notice him, he's already too close.

"I knew they'd leave you alone eventually," Javier says with a bloody smile, gore coating his hands, mouth, and chest.

Well, I didn't see that coming.

RHYS

West and I swiftly and silently make our way up the short staircase to the loft, West in the lead since his night vision is much better than mine. With my light, I can make out the watered-down blood sitting in puddles on the hardwood floor. The sprinklers have trickled off, no longer pelting us with freezing-cold water.

He moves to check the bathroom while I work on clearing the bedroom. The room appears empty at first, but I'd feel a hell of a lot better if we could find Javier and Carver. That, and figure out who brought a fucking Revenant to the party.

Catching sight of a shoe, I find Carver half-sitting, half-sprawled on the floor behind the club chair in the corner. He's gasping shallowly, doing his best to try and talk, but given the foamy bubbles coming out of his mouth, his lung is punctured.

That doesn't stop his mouth from moving, his eyes wild, desperate.

Or I should say "eye."

His arms and face are deeply slashed, enough to know that unless he can heal from it, Carver is likely going to lose his right eye. Four deep gashes span from his left shoulder to his belly, and in a circle around his heart, he has five distinct puncture wounds. The Revenant must have been interrupted in the process of ripping out his heart.

Lucky bastard.

Letting out a low whistle, I feel West's approach as I yank a throw blanket from the chair and try to stem the flow of blood.

"Ja-Javier. Re... re... re..." Carver gasps but loses consciousness before he can get the words out.

This whole thing is wrong. First the security breach, then the Revenant, and we haven't found Javi. This situation has "fucked" written all over it. By the expression on West's face, he's thinking the exact thing I am.

"Can he even heal from this?" I ask because wraith anatomy is not exactly something I've studied up on.

"Best case, yes, but it'll take several days. Worst case?" He shakes his head.

My jaw clenches. "You find Javi?"

"No."

That is not a good answer—especially since there is only one wraith unaccounted for. It doesn't take a rocket scientist to figure out who did this. "We need to get back to Aidan and Aurelia and get the fuck out of here."

We don't even make it to the first step before I feel the ripping sensation in my chest. Shock has me stumbling as I reach for my ribs, my hands coming away with the warm wetness of fresh blood.

Aurelia, I think as the already-dark world goes black.

15

AURELIA

Gasping awake, the cold instantly seeps into my bones. My clothes are rough against my skin, stiff with dried blood. The bite of the shackles encircle both my wrists and ankles, my arms stretched above my head, already half-numb from the position. I try, but I can't move my hands or feet more than a few inches. The stainless-steel table I'm chained to looks like a morgue slab. The clank of the metal on metal causes a shudder to shake its way up my spine.

Well, I've been here before.

The panic attack barreling its way through me is nothing new, and it takes roughly an age to get under control. Well, and a teeny, tiny nap as I pass out from hyperventilation. But, hey, I'm being held hostage. I get one freebie meltdown, *right*?

Consciousness takes its sweet, merry time coming back. I know this because now the room has people in it. I can't see or hear them, but I *know* they're here. I'm willing to go out on a limb here and say some form of torture is about to start.

At this juncture, I scratch the life goal of never being tortured again at the top of my wish list.

The barren room is decidedly gray with windowless cinderblock and buzzing florescent lights hanging from the ceiling. Moisture crawls up the walls, the scent of mold and death invading my nostrils.

A cell, my brain supplies, slow on the uptake. *Yippee. I've always wanted to die in prison.*

A soldier appears in my line of sight, and it requires a fuck-ton of self-possession to tamp down my fear. Especially since he has a very large Morganite blade in his hand.

Is that big of a blade really necessary?

Apparently so, because he's using it to cut away my clothes, leaving me in the draft—the pervert. He's quick and efficient, removing my shirt and jeans before I can get over the shock of what he's doing. When he gets to the point of the festivities where he tries to cut the middle of my bra—that's where I snap out of it.

Putting an Aegis on a metal table with steal bonds is a very bad plan. I've never been happier to completely fry someone in my life.

I shove the electricity from my chest, coating my flesh, allowing it to travel down and out of me through the table all the way to the hand the idiot rests on the edge. It's as if I'm touching him with a live wire, disrupting the rhythm of his heart, burning him from the inside out.

A dark smile curls my lips when I see the wetness running down his leg before he collapses. The memory of the bastard pissing himself will probably never get old—even if the smell of charred flesh fills my nose.

But letting that bit of myself go free wakes up the aches and pains in my body. I've squandered too much energy, and now I have the added fun of trying to get out of my shackles.

It takes a while to work myself up to it, but I manage to dislocate my right thumb, just barely holding onto my gorge as it rises in my throat. The smell of flambeed soldier and his loose bowels does nothing to me, but dislocating one measly joint, and I'm ready to toss my cookies.

I squeeze my right hand out of the cuff before snapping my thumb back into place.

Don't puke. Don't puke.

Now I've reached a dilemma. I still have three limbs trapped, and the thought of dislocating another thumb—*nope. I'll wait a minute.*

"It took longer than I anticipated for you to dispatch him," a voice calls, and my already-topsy-turvy stomach nearly loses it.

I'd know that voice anywhere.

Iva.

The woman I've feared for more years than I care to count saunters into my line of sight. Outfitted in a pristine white dress that clings to her slender frame, she surveys the fallen guard as if she can actually see him. Once, I'd thought white had been a symbol of purity, but the way she wears it, the color will always remind me of death. It makes sense that everything—even her hair—carries the trademark shade.

Everything but her eyes.

A century ago, she wore dark, green-tinted spectacles to hide the hollow sockets where her eyes used to be. Now, brown prosthetic ones fill the space, their odd ability to follow my movements unnerving.

"Sorry to disappoint. I didn't know we were having a party," I say referring to her gown. "I would have dressed up."

Iva bends to scoop up the Morganite blade, locating it as if the prosthetics were real.

"I think your clothing is the least of your worries, dear," she warns, her Irish lilt setting my teeth on edge. She tosses the blade from one hand to the other, taunting me. "What you should be worried about is that pesky Aegis taint you have in your blood. I've worked very hard to eradicate that irksome little faction. I'll not have it passing down your line. Oh. That's right, there won't be anyone else in your line, now, will there? No matter." She shrugs as the knife's tip touches the skin of my inner thigh.

It doesn't break the skin, only indents the flesh as she glides the blade down my leg. I try my best not to shake, but fear—*fuck*—it makes me lose myself.

"Now, do I bleed it out of you?" Iva muses. "Or do I use other ways to rid you of that blasted power?" Her eyes squint in consideration, her red-painted mouth screwing up to the side.

I'm pretty sure whatever way she chooses, I'm not going to like it.

Being known for tossing spells around like candy, Iva is not the woman I want experimenting on me. She sets the knife down and places her slender hands against the skin of my face.

Nope. Don't like this already.

When the chanting starts, I can't focus on anything else but the pain. It's like being covered in fire ants, or battery acid, or fire—if fire could actually burn me. Iva's fingertips dig into my cheeks, gouging my skin, the bite of it almost pleasurable compared to whatever spell she's casting.

I can't think.

I can't breathe.

All I can do is lay there and pray this agony isn't killing Rhys, too.

I WAKE UP IN THE GRAY, STERILE, ROOM FROM HELL—*AGAIN*—seriously contemplating how many times I'm going to pass out in this hellhole.

At least I'm alone.

My cotton-filled head is blissfully without pain, though. That or those particular receptors in my noggin decided to say, "fuck it" and bailed on me while I was passed out. Either way, I'm counting it as a win.

I take advantage of my numbed state and dislocate my left thumb.

Nothing. No pain at all.

Groggily, I hope Rhys isn't the recipient of it all. That would suck. I shimmy the cuff off and pop my thumb back into place. Bringing my arms down, I shake the blood back into them. While I can't feel pain right now, I do notice the muted, pins-and-needles sensation of the loss of circulation.

Now I have the arduous task of stretching my body off this table to attempt to reach the downed soldier on the floor. He's lying in a lump where he stumbled away near the end of the table, wearing the traditional garb of a steel breastplate held on by straps of leather and leather combat skirt.

That's it. No under clothing, no tunic, nada.

I always thought it was a waste to have the soldiers dressed as eye candy when the oracles were blind.

The key to the shackles is clipped to the leather-studded belt holding his skirt up. I feel the chain pulling on my ankle, but I'm not bleeding, so I figure all's well.

Just. One. More. Inch.

Fumbling the keys, I manage to catch them before they fall. Now I get to do the semi-hilarious half-crab walk back on the table. Out of the shackles within seconds, I stand, getting my first real look at myself. I'm practically a horror movie reject in my blood-covered bra and panties.

If my friends could see me now, I'd likely get laughed at for days. My thoughts go to them, and I hope everyone is okay. I scoop up the blade and quietly pad over to the door, the adrenaline of impending freedom waking me up a little bit.

The door is unlocked, but I shove the keys into my bra for lack of a better place to put them, snatch the Morganite blade from the table, and make my way toward the light. The hallway is at odds with the cell I just vacated. The rich wood paneling is tastefully adorned with paintings older than Iva. Several doors line the corridor, and my biggest fear is someone walking out of one of them, catching me before I can get the fuck out of here.

The silhouette of a figure moving up ahead casts against the wood, but before they see me, I move into the shadow of a doorway. The small inlet in the wood is not quite enough space for me to hide, though. Then he turns the corner, moving down the corridor, shooting a glance over his shoulder. Even with his face half-turned away from me, I recognize him.

It's tough to forget someone stabbing you in the chest—that's for sure.

Javier saunters closer, and blindly, I reach behind me, praying the hinges are silent. My back to the opening, I thank whatever deity I need to that the door was unlocked.

Glancing around in the darkness, I see almost nothing. No movement, no breathing. The smell is awful, though, as if someone or something has died here. I step farther into the gloom but leave the door ajar. Javier is moving toward me, and I'm sure he'll come to investigate either the smell or the cracked door at some point.

Sure enough, he stops at the entrance to this cell. I don't blink—I don't even breathe as I wait for him to cross the threshold. Tightening my grip on the blade, my impending vengeance curls my mouth into a gruesome smile, and I'm still grinning when he walks fully into the room. Keeping the feral pull to my mouth, I efficiently cut off his head before turning him to ash.

Fire, one. Revenant, zero.

Through the dying embers of Javier's corpse, I glimpse a figure on the bed. A woman. She's unmoving, her matted brown hair covering her face. I check her and note she is not true dead. From what I sense, though, she'll be out for a few more days.

Dead weight.

I can't help her now, but I swear to myself when I get out of here, I'm bringing people back with me to free her and anyone else imprisoned here. Guilt floods me as I make my way out of the room and down the rest of the hallway.

Leaving the woman behind feels wrong. Wrong in a way I can't name or quantify.

Sticking to the wall—mostly for support—I come to

a large landing. One side leads to a grand staircase, and the opposite side is a service stairwell—the commotion of a kitchen bubbling up the steps. Keeping to the shadows, I skirt the circular space and pad down the servants' stairs.

Of all the places for me to go, a kitchen is probably the last route I should take. It's bustling with people preparing a meal, and a bloody, underwear-clad woman, is going to go over like a fart at High Tea.

I wait in the shadows trying to decide if taking a hostage is necessary for me to get out of here, or if the workers are too busy to notice me. Hoping for the best, I choose option two. Crouching low, I make it fifteen of the twenty feet to the door before a very young gentry woman notices me.

She may look young, but her gaze is haunted. She knows what's chained within these walls. I put my finger to my lips, and she nods, looking away as if she'd seen nothing.

The next five feet are simple, and the door makes nary a squeak as it opens and shuts. I flee the warmth of the house to the cold, damp, darkness of the night. I'm not sure where the hell I am, but the weather and tree line suggest the Pacific Northwest. The house sits atop a lush foothill of a verdant mountain. Somewhere in

Oregon, possibly, and I wonder if it's the same village I grew up in.

These woods were my playground so many years ago, and it doesn't take a psychic to foresee a pair of cut-up, dirt-covered, feet in my future.

The forest is far louder than I expect. The trees rustle in the wind, bugs trill and chirp in the fading light, but I'm still the loudest thing here. As carefully as I step, and as slowly as I'm walking, I still make a huge freaking racket. I stop, crouching in the high grass as I attempt to sense if anyone is following me. My head is still filled with cotton, and I feel nothing.

Picking up the pace, I figure if slow is loud, then I might as well go fast.

The descent becomes sharp, and before I know it, the trees are starting to thin. The precipice of a cliff emerges into view, and I scramble to slow down. My fingers scrabble in the dirt before an errant root allows me to skid to a halt at the edge of a fucking mountain.

Breathless, I nearly start giggling at the utter absurdity of it all. Especially since from what I can figure, I'm only left with two choices. I can attempt to climb the steep incline I just skidded down, praying no one from the Legion house is in the forest looking for me, or I can try to phase and coast down this cliff.

This also requires a fair bit of hope—especially since I don't know how to fly.

While I do have wings, my primary feathers were cut by a Morganite blade when I was tortured by Iva so long ago. Those essential feathers—the ones that could have allowed me to soar—will never grow back.

That said, in the last one hundred and sixty years, I've had a lot of time on my hands, and studying bird anatomy is a hobby of mine. A bird can still coast with their secondary feathers, and I have those.

I might as well try it. It's not like the fall will kill me.

The burn of transformation races over my flesh. The fire is first, coating my hands, up my limbs, to my torso. The flame only stings for a second before it starts to heal. The cuts and scrapes on my feet and legs are closing—my thumbs no longer swollen and tight.

The wings are next—bones crunch and crack before the added weight of my feathers rest upon my shoulders. It's been too long. I stretch, shaking them to adjust to their size. They've grown a little in the last ten years or so—as they are known to do—but I don't think they'll get much bigger. Or at least I hope not. The wings hang down my back and reach the forest floor—the tips slightly bent and dragging.

The colors have changed over the years. As a child, they were fluffy and white, with the barest hint of yellow on the coverts. As a teenager, they were bright orange and yellow. Now they're almost blood-red at the tips of the feathers, bleeding from a candy-apple to amber.

I stretch them out, flapping them once to catch the air with the feathers. In theory, this hair-brained idea should work as long as I have enough room to coast.

Shoring my fears, I hurdle myself off the edge of the cliff. The ground rushes at me rapidly, and I'm positive I'm about to go *splat* before the feathers catch a downdraft, and I glide the rest of the way down. I circle my feet in a running motion like skydivers before they land, but I fail miserably and completely biff the landing, eating dirt like a pro.

Well, at least I didn't die.

The loud shuffle of footsteps sounds to my left, and I crack an eyelid to spy my impending fate. I'm still dazed, too busy coughing up forest bracken to even react. Three pairs of black leather motorcycle boots race into my line of sight—two large pairs and one small, dainty pair. The small ones are tapping a single foot as if irritated.

Craning my head, I blearily gaze up at Rhys, Evan, and West—each standing with their arms crossed, their expressions murderous.

It is completely possible I should have waited before jumping off a cliff.

Whoops.

16

RHYS

Pissed-off energy radiates through the SUV, but as mad as I am, the relief warming my chest holds me together. With Aurelia safely in my arms, it's tough to remember just how angry I am that she launched herself off a fucking cliff.

Seven days, I think, pressing a kiss to her hair. *Seven whole days without her.*

How did I survive these last few decades apart when seven days has been the highest form of torture? Maybe it's because I never really had her.

Maybe it's because she was never really mine. The thought of going another day without her by my side has my heart falling to my stomach.

Aurelia had been held for a full week before she escaped—six days of which, she was unconscious. The second she opened her eyes, that knowledge etched its way into my soul.

None of it made any sense.

Typically, when I "die" so does she. When I'm hurt, we both bleed. But this time was different. This time, I got medical care immediately, while she was stuck bleeding and alone in the middle of enemy territory.

That had never happened—not in a century and a half—and the absence of her presence in my mind was like losing a bit of my soul. She'd always been there in my head: the bits and pieces of emotions, her needs, her wants, but it was so much more now—our bond only growing stronger since we finally came together.

I knew where she was the instant she opened her eyes, and the five of us got on a plane—not that our rescue attempt was necessary.

The first day she woke up, she broke out, and I don't know if that's scary or sexy as hell. Preferring to lean toward sexy rather than think of the alternative, I gather her more securely in my arms and stare out the windshield.

The closest airstrip to the Legion compound is in Eugene, and from there we rented a car to get to the isolated property hidden in the middle of the Willamette National Forest. Said vehicle is filled to the brim with a level of unease I have yet to experience in my lifetime.

A wave of irate energy radiates from Aidan and Ian who are stuffed in the cramped third-row seat. The brothers are still kicking themselves because they hadn't realized that Javier had been a traitorous Revenant. Well, that, and the fact that we left them in the SUV in search of my woman.

In the front seats, West and Evan's emotions match the brothers, but according to Evan's grumblings, it's just because we didn't get to kill anyone. And me? I'm trying to forget that I watched Aurelia jump off a fucking cliff on clipped wings.

The palpable silence continues until we reach a bed and breakfast on the way to Eugene. The agreement to stop to let Aurelia get cleaned up and dressed in something other than blood-covered underwear is done mostly with grumbles and truncated grunts.

It's probably fucked in the head that seeing her bloody, half-naked, and armed made my dick stand at attention, but I can't make myself give a shit. I have every intention of utilizing our rented room's full potential and fucking my woman on every available surface until the ache in my chest goes away.

I don't care if we need to get as far away as possible from Iva and her fucking soldiers.

I don't care if we have bigger problems.

I need her.

I need to feel for myself that she's safe—that this isn't all a dream.

Sneaking her in is easy, the bevy of wraiths in attendance giving us plenty of options as to who will ferry her into the sleepy B&B unnoticed. But being out of touching distance of her does something to me. I'm practically shaking by the time I get to our room, the call of the running water pushing my feet toward the cracked bathroom door.

The simple bathroom is decked out in shades of white, the steam from the falling water making the whole space seem almost like a mirage. Behind the waffle-weave shower curtain, Aurelia is wet, naked, and soapy, the draining puddle at her feet tinted pink from the spent blood rinsing from her skin.

The illogical urge to fuck her against the shower wall nearly overtakes me, and when she meets my burning gaze, I know she feels it, too. Not trying to rationalize it, I start stripping off my clothes, and I'm in the shower without saying a word.

Not that words are necessary.

The only essential thing right now is the connection

we share—the need. I don't wait—I just lift her against the cold tile, grab my cock, and line it up with her center, thrusting into her to the hilt.

"Yes," she hisses, her fingers roughly threading into my hair and yanking my lips to hers.

Our tongues collide, and I couldn't give a single shit about the rest of the world. It could all come crashing around our ears for all I care. All I need is her body in my arms, her taste on my tongue, and her slick, wet heat enveloping my cock.

She writhes, urging me to fuck her harder, faster, more. The noises she's making—*Fates*—I love those fucking noises. They are one part moan, one part whimper—like she's begging without ever saying a word. Snapping my hips harder, I give her what she's asking for.

Aurelia's breath hitches, her fingernails gouging the flesh on my shoulders, almost breaking the skin. The bite of pain races down my spine, and I can't keep my pace, can't hold in my growl. I pump my hips faster and faster until her wail of a moan signals her orgasm. The squeeze of her inner muscles nearly have me following her over the edge.

But I'm not ready to let her go yet.

Lifting her off my length, I spin her around, pressing her steaming body against the freezing tile as I enter her from behind. Aurelia's tight as a vise this way, and my release races down my spine. Reaching around, I clutch her lush breast in my hand and move my other down to play with her pretty little clit. Pinching her nipple and clit at the same time, I wrench a scream from her as she comes again, ripping my orgasm from me. My groan is muffled when I sink my teeth into the flesh at her shoulder, just shy of breaking the skin, earning me a shuddering whimper.

Gently, I pull out, turning her so I can kiss her soft lips. Then I do what I should have done before and take care of her. Thanking the Fates for giant water heaters, I leisurely help wash her hair and body. It takes all my effort to be gentle, because something is eating at me, and I figure we both know what it is.

Shutting off the water, I step out and pluck the fluffy towel from its hook. I dry her off, wrapping her in the thick cotton like I wish I could have last week.

You should have stayed with her, I scold myself as I roughly yank the other towel from its perch and wrap it around my waist. *She got taken because you left her behind. What kind of soldier are you?*

Who knows what happened to her in those seven days? We found her nearly naked, preferring to launch herself off a cliff than face whatever lay behind her. None of that could be good.

Aurelia was semi-manic after her brief flying episode, and it took nearly an hour to get her to phase back. Maybe it was the trauma, or maybe it was because it's been forever since she'd last phased. In that hour, she told us everything—or what I hoped was everything, given the lack of clothing when she escaped.

As she rambled, she paced, her jittery hands flailing as she spoke, her flames coating her body as she burned the grass beneath her feet. All the while, I got my first good look at her clipped wings, and it took every ounce of strength I possessed to clamp down my rage.

I thought I knew everything there was to know about Aurelia Constantine, but I had no idea how wrong I was—had no idea that something so vital had been ripped from her, too.

And her wings aren't the only thing Iva has stolen from her.

The way she told it, Iva was under the impression she could remove the Aegis side of Aurelia's abilities. The mere mention of this had my blood running cold. Hell, it still does. Because if Iva did remove it, one leg of Aurelia's protection is dust.

And if she didn't?

Aurelia's Aegis could return at any time.

She could hurt someone.

Kill someone.

But more? Neither of us know what it means for her visions.

I'm still working up the courage to talk to her about our next move when she puts a hand on my arm, halting my search for a blow dryer.

"Stop, baby," she says, staying my hands as they raid the last cabinet. She knows something is still bothering me, and it doesn't take a psychic to figure it out since I'm slamming the cabinet doors like an idiot. "If you want to know something, just ask. If you want to tell me something, just tell me. Whatever it is, I can take it."

I can't look at her. I don't want whatever is on my face to make her lie to me.

"Did anything else happen in there?" I croak, not wanting to know but asking all the same. "Anything that you didn't want to say in front of the others? Like why you escaped wearing only your underwear?"

Asking these questions is the most moronic thing I can think of. If her answers are what I fear, I'll be going back to that compound to murder anyone who so much as touched her.

"No, baby," she replies, squeezing my arm so I meet her gaze. "There was a soldier who tried to get frisky, but my last act as an Aegis fried him from the inside out. No one but Iva touched me."

The anger that throbbed through me slides away. "My bloodthirsty wife. I like it."

"It's a part of my charm," she says with a grin. "And wife, huh?"

Latching onto the soft cotton, I rest my hip against the counter as I pull her to me. "We've been bonded for a hundred and sixty years, Gorgeous. Might as well call you what you are to me. After almost losing you, I want it all. I want to call you my wife. I never want us to be apart. I am in it, and I need you there with me." Moving my hands to her face, I cup her jaw and meet those beautifully odd eyes. "If you want the party and pretty dress, you can have it, but it doesn't change the fact you've been my wife for a very long time."

Lucien might have been her husband once upon a time, but our bond eclipses any claims they made to one another. In our world, that marriage was annulled the second I accepted those rites.

It's just taken this long for her to join me.

And yes, it's fast. Of course she might balk at the idea of us moving at warp speed.

But I have to be honest with her.

A tremulous smile stretches her lips, and Aurelia traces a finger down my scars. "I want the party and the pretty dress. And a ring. A big honking, sparkly, competes-with-the-sun-sized ring. But later. Deal?"

The joy that hits me at her easy agreement nearly takes my breath.

"Deal," I growl before taking her mouth in a fierce kiss.

"Anything else?" she asks when we break for a breath.

"How do you want to play this?" I ask, moving to the next facet of my anxiety. "You escaped, yes, but we didn't win. Now you're down a power, and we don't know when or if it's coming back. If *she's* coming back. We need to decide where we're going."

She considers this for about half a second.

"I want to go home," Aurelia admits, her pale gaze no longer meeting mine. "I want to sleep in my own bed. Evan, John, and their entire crew can come with us if they want to. I have the room. My place is secluded, secure, and has my studio. I need to shake this off and think of a new plan to get that bitch." She places her hands against my chest and pushes away. "There were prisoners there, Rhys. Who knows how many there are? We have to stop Iva. And we have to save those people."

Holing up in her house? It's not a bad plan. "I think we can do that. I know the wraiths will help. And you're right—we can't let her take more lives. I'll talk to the others, see if they're onboard."

She nods and moves me aside to grab the dryer,

getting to work on her heavy fall of hair as I pull my clothes back on. Then I leave the warmth of the bathroom to collect a fresh set of clothes for her and whatever else Evan has scrounged up in the last hour. Opening the door, I find the manic pixie holding three bulging shopping bags.

"Go talk to the boys," she says, shoving past me into our room. "She wants to go home, right?"

"How'd you know?" I ask over the roar of the hair dryer.

"She hasn't painted in two weeks. That's like cutting off a limb for her," she answers like I'm an idiot, dumping the fresh clothes out of the bags and removing the tags. "Her house is secure—maybe more than Dad's —*and* she has more weapons."

That has me taking a step back. "How could she *possibly* have more weapons?"

A frown mars my friend's face as she stares at me like I'm a special kind of stupid. "She's been dreaming of war and death for almost two centuries, Rhys. That makes a girl mighty paranoid."

She's got me there.

Leaving her to it, I close the door behind me to go talk to the rest of the men. Aidan answers when I knock on their door, barring my way, likely still mad at me for telling him to stay with his brother.

Dumbass.

"Get over it, dude," I grumble, shouldering past him.

West looks up from his perusal of his phone. "She wants to go home?"

How he knows this already, I have no clue, but I nod anyway. "Yep. After what she's been through, I'll give her whatever she wants, so..."

"It's not a bad plan," Ian agrees. "I'm told it's secure and stocked better than an armory. Thoughts?"

"Why not?" Aidan grouses. "No one else has come up with anything. With Javier's betrayal, so many of our safe houses are gone. We have no idea how many locations have been compromised. Her house?" He lifts a shoulder in indifference. "It might be the only place for us."

Then I guess we have a plan.

WHILE AURELIA'S HOUSE IS MODEST COMPARED TO JOHN'S, the five-bedroom, five-bath home is nothing if not comfortable. Wide picture windows display the mountains beyond, the smooth plastered walls painted a soothing green that reminds me of Aurelia's eyes. The wide French doors lead to a wraparound deck, but it's the vaulted ceilings that are the real showpiece. Peaked at an incredible slope, they're gently broken up by giant wooden beams that constantly pull my gaze upward.

And the pillows.

Dainty lace ones, medium solid ones, and large printed ones reside on every squashy armchair, couch, and side chair. Aurelia's house was made for loafing—each piece selected for maximum comfort.

Lounging on the chocolate-brown leather sectional, to the untrained eye I appear at ease. My head practically drowning in pillows, I watch her work at her easel. I may seem relaxed, but I'm stressed the fuck out on the inside, thinking about all that Evan has told me.

The both of us—hell, even John searched—but we can't find a single person that can help us bring her Aegis power back. The same power that saved her from the insanity of vision after vision, death after death. We thought she was safe.

Oh, how wrong we were.

No matter who we talk to, they don't seem to have enough juice to help, or they refuse to go against Iva. Our Primary's reign of terror has filtered through every species of the Ethereal.

And it shows. Clawing fingers of dread pull at me as I look at her work.

Aurelia sits perched on a bar stool, her withered

frame hunched as she feverishly slaps paint on the canvas. I brought it down from the kitchen island two days ago when her legs refused to hold her up.

Too tired to stand but too amped to sleep, she remains on that stool, creating image after image filled with nightmares. Her paintings blend abstract splashes of color with the realism of portraits. When she does talk, she tells me what they mean—which herald of death they portray. But as the days pass, each painting becomes more and more haunting.

Each death more chilling than the last.

Her hand moves blindingly fast as the black and grey and deep purple meld together to make a horrified face. The picture is a close-up of a woman's eyes, the expression in them pleading. The eyes are tearing with purple blood instead of saline. But the blood isn't blood at all. It appears to be morphing into the reflection of the person that killed her.

Honestly, she's scaring the shit out of me.

When she does manage to nod off, she startles awake, screaming, and the longer we're here, the less she sleeps. But the lack of sleep is not the only toll Iva's machinations are taking on her body.

In just a few short days, Aurelia has practically withered under the strain—her cheekbones sharp, her face creased with exhaustion and worry. I can't get her to eat, and her body is shrinking by the minute, dropping weight she can't afford to lose. Purple shadows have taken up residence under her eyes, and her voice has gone from lively and sarcastic to a half-dead monotone.

So here I sit, watching my woman waste away as I try to come up with another way to help.

Problem is, I've called in every favor I have stocked up from every witch, wraith, and warlock I know. No one can help us.

Her Aegis protected her—and now?

I worry there isn't anything anyone can do.

17

AURELIA

A young man and woman are driving a vehicle on a dark road. It isn't a new car. Duct tape fails to hold the stuffing inside the driver's headrest, errant fluffs of foam spill from a rip in the tape. A faint knocking comes from the weakly chugging engine. The windows are down, most likely because the AC no longer works, the wind from the summer night whipping their hair to and fro.

The young man is thin to the point of starvation with dark blue-black circles under his eyes and a wary, haunted look on his face. He couldn't be more than fifteen at a push, but the few years he's spent on this earth have not been kind. His joints are knobby and pointed, his chin sharp and dotted *with acne and scars of abuse. His lip is split, and he has a blooming purple bruise on his left cheek.*

The woman is crying, clutching the boy's hand in a vise grip. Her hands are raw, the fingernails bloody and jagged, some even ripped from the nail beds. Her dark hair is matted against her skull—greasy and filthy, clumped with blood and dirt.

Someone has beaten her severely—her left eye black and closing, her nose bloody, swollen and crooked from an obvious break. She is also hugely pregnant—the thinness of her limbs making her burgeoning womb appear larger than it is. Ridges of her ribs peak through the tear at the breast of her dirty blouse.

They erratically drive down a mountain—the switchbacks making the tires skid from the speed. The tires slide over the road, over the double-yellow lines, and into the oncoming lane. The young man overcorrects the trajectory of the puttering car, sliding once again into the gravel of the shoulder. They pass a well-lit diner, the light of the sign casting a yellow, sickly glow upon the woman's face. She cries out in horror, clutching her belly with her mangled fingers.

And then the blood comes.

Gushes of scarlet pour from between her legs, soaking through her tattered skirt and the battered seat below her. Her face goes gray from the blood loss—even the bruises leaching of color—and she loses consciousness within a few seconds.

The boy slams the accelerator down, desperately trying to make it to their destination. His eyes leak frustrated tears, and he begs the woman to wake up, his screams and pleas growing louder and louder as the minutes pass.

He pushes the poor car as fast as it can go, but he's too late. By the time the bright hospital lights have cast their glow on the beat-up rattrap of a car, she's stopped breathing.

He screeches into the emergency bay, the car skidding sideways as it grinds to a stop. He screams for help as he flies out his door, hobbling to the passenger side. He yanks open the door, shaking the woman by the shoulders, before unbuckling her seatbelt and attempting to pull her from the car.

Doctors and nurses flood from the doors, pulling the woman from her seat, shoving her on a gurney, and rushing her inside.

But they are all too late.

No matter how hard the doctors work, they can't save them.

I'M SHAKEN AWAKE FOR THE FOURTH TIME TONIGHT. RHYS engulfs my sweaty, shaking body into a giant bear hug, his warm skin on mine easing me until I notice red on the sheets. Immediately, I jump up to check myself and the bed for blood. There is nothing on my belly or underwear, but my hands are bloody from my fingernails ripping into my palms in my sleep.

Dammit.

Well, at least I'm not screaming this time. I wish I could call that a win, but I can't. I plop back down on the mattress.

"This shit has got to stop. I want you to take the sleeping pills, Gorgeous," he pleads with me as he grabs the full glass I neglected after the second wake-up call tonight.

"I don't want to," I say in a small, feeble voice.

I hate that voice.

I wish I weren't so tired.

I wish I weren't so weak.

I wish I would sleep and see nothing.

My sanity is frayed, unraveling swiftly with each vision, and I don't have the strength to re-braid the ropes.

"This is the fourth time you've woken up tonight," Rhys reminds me, "and it's only midnight. You're not even asleep for more than twenty minutes before the next vision starts. If a pill helps, you need to take it."

His eyes are weary, his dark-brown hair disheveled from his restless night. I'm hurting him—whether it's from my lack of sleep or my fingers ripping into the flesh of my hands.

I'm hurting him. And I don't want to.

"I'm scared," I mutter, my voice wobbling. "What if I get stuck?"

Fucking tears. They slip and slide down my face in pitiful little rivulets. *When did I get so weak?*

"Let's just try it once," he offers, "and if you hate it or if it doesn't work, then we can stop. But we have to do something. I can't watch you in agony and not do something, Gorgeous."

I have to do this. I have to try. For him.

"I'm sorry you're in pain, too. I'll take the pill." I sigh, twisting the sheets in my fingers. "You'll stay with me, though, right?"

"Where else would I want to be?" he replies before dropping a gentle kiss to my shoulder.

"Okay." I nod, taking the tall glass of water and a tiny pink pill.

Here goes nothing.

A YOUNG BOY—NO BIGGER THAN FIVE—JUMPS IN PUDDLES ON *a sidewalk. The gray sky beyond him threatens more rain, but the boy is enjoying his reprieve, bouncing from one tiny puddle to the next.*

His mother watches him from under the cover of a porch awning—her curly black hair pulled into a messy bun atop her head. She's dressed plainly in jeans and a T-shirt—the pale-gray cardigan covering her slim shoulders matching the overcast sky. The house is modest but not shabby, the lawn groomed, the shutters freshly painted. The window boxes are blooming with summer flowers, trailing pink and purple blossoms over the sides.

The neighborhood is situated at the base of a mountain range—the verdant hills broken up with jutting bedrock, nearly blotting out the light from the cloudy sky.

She's sitting on the first step, waiting for the boy to get his fill of the outdoors. She has a thick book on her lap, and she is shuffling index cards in her hands, furiously studying. She glances up every few seconds, though, checking on her son.

His little face is screwed up in concentration as he considers the next jump. He counts to three, and away he goes, his bright-yellow rain boots splashing in the water. The vinyl of his raincoat squeaks as he flaps his arms, making boom *and* zoom *noises with his loud little boy mouth.*

It has rained so much in the last few weeks. Almost every single day has been filled with constant deluges of falling water.

The boy doesn't feel the rumble, but the mother does. She tosses aside her book and notes, the white index cards fluttering about the lawn like leaves until they're swept away by the roaring tide of a flash flood.

She makes it to her son, but she's too late to save him.

She's too late to save herself.

He clings to her, and she works so hard, kicking her legs and clawing the water with her free hand to try and keep their heads above the surface.

She tires quickly and then fails in her endeavor altogether when they're slammed into a parked SUV. The torrent rushes up and over the vehicle, but the mother and son are pinned beneath the surface, fighting, and clawing for air in the freezing flood.

A young woman walks alone down a darkened street,

shivering in rapidly falling temperatures of a summer night in the mountains.

Slight and blonde, she strides with purpose, her shoulders tensed. She's wearing an old diner waitress uniform—said diner is fading in the background as she makes her way to the lit bus stop ahead. The diner's pale-yellow sign is now off, but the blue lettering still reads "Sunflower Café."

She stops and removes the heavy backpack from her shoulders, pulling a lime-green hoodie from the pack. Her bag is stuffed full of clothes and books, a key chain mace canister attached to the zipper.

Her bulging pack is still at her feet when the man approaches her from behind, a pristinely folded white cloth in his hand. He uses it to cover her face, and her struggle is over quickly as she loses consciousness. The man is well-groomed, wearing a starched navy-blue button-up and pressed khakis. His brown hair is carefully combed, and his leather loafers are polished to a high shine. He looks like a deacon of a church, or a dentist, or an insurance salesman.

The man drags her from the street toward a wooded area beyond, snatching up her backpack as he goes, her tired pink Chucks making tiny ruts in the gravel shoulder of the once-busy road.

He takes little care with the woman as he drags her body in the mud and bracken of the forest floor—the limbs scratching at her exposed skin. He stops in a clearing, placing her body just so before heading to a nearby stump. Resting on the dirt is a silver, hard-sided suitcase.

The stranger carefully places the case on the stump and clicks open the locks, pulling a black instrument case from the felt. He then dons a pair of disposable gloves, snapping the rubber for the perfect fit. Slipping a pair of pliers from their loop, he opens her mouth, and begins ripping each and every tooth from her head.

The woman rouses around tooth fifteen, her pitiful protestations dulled to a gurgle as she chokes on the blood running down her throat. The stranger carefully removes the white cloth from his pocket, drowning out her moans with more chloroform.

Finishing his task, he removes the remainder of the woman's teeth. He then drags her to a freshly dug hole in the ground, tossing her unconscious body into the earth. The man removes a small bottle of lighter fluid from his pocket and drenches her body with it—squeezing the yellow container until every last drop has fallen from the tiny spigot.

He throws the plastic in with the body along with her backpack before removing a pack of matches from his other pocket, studying them with interest. The script is delicate and flowery, the name of a local inn emblazoned across the front.

The stranger lights the book and tosses it in, the flames

igniting with a whoosh.

The unassuming man studies the flames for a long while, observing the woman's body burn to cinders in her roughly hewn grave. When the poor woman's body is reduced to embers, he takes the collapsible shovel from his suitcase, using it to fill the hole with loose earth. With the flat end of the blade, he tamps down the dirt. When he's done, he drags broken tree limbs and fallen brush over the mound, perfectly concealing the shallow grave.

The stranger returns to the stump, pulling a black velvet drawstring from his roll of tools. Carefully, he places each of the woman's teeth in the bag before pulling the string closed and carefully placing it in the front pocket of his khakis.

Walking from the clearing, the stranger heads away from the busy main road to a rough dirt rut where a shiny SUV is parked. He rounds the vehicle with his tools in tow, smiling all the while—patting his pocket as he goes.

MY EYES OPEN TO SUNLIGHT STREAMING IN THROUGH THE blinds. Rhys is cuddled up to my back, his arm thrown over my hip—the turquoise sheet pulled up to my chest. His warmth would be comforting, maybe, but now I can't find comfort in anything anymore.

I don't move for a full minute, neglecting to speak, gently lifting his hand off me and sliding out of bed. Padding to the master bath, I carefully close the door before turning on the shower taps, and promptly losing the contents of my stomach.

I know those mountains. I drive down them every single time I head into Denver.

I know that motel. It's two miles away from my house.

I know that diner. I've had lunch there more times than I can count.

I know what this is.

This is the death of every good soul around me. These are souls that need to pass on. The souls I would direct a gentry toward.

This is what I would feel if I never had the Aegis in the first place. This is what a seer really is. No wonder seer's just line up to get their eyes cut out. If this is what I saw every night before maturity, I'd do anything to make it stop.

I still might.

Shaking, I brush my teeth, noticing the graying gauntness of my face in the vanity mirror.

I can survive this, I think as I rinse and spit into the sink. Stripping off my underwear, I toss them in the hamper and step under the scalding spray.

On autopilot, I shower, rinsing the horrors from last night off my skin, thinking of nothing as the world swirls away to blackness.

18

RHYS

The midday sun shines across my face, and I wake wrapped around a still-sleeping Aurelia. Her back is to me, her damp hair tickles my nose as I sigh in relief.

She slept. Thank the Fates.

I drop a kiss to her shoulder and the tender skin of her neck, noticing a change to her scent. She smells different somehow, almost like aged parchment and baby powder—the faint cloying scent fills me with unease. I don't like it and wonder how I could politely ask her to switch body washes to whatever she was using when we first made love.

She stirs, but her controlled stillness bores a hole of

worry in my gut. I try to brush it off as the effects of the sleeping medication.

Aurelia rouses, rubbing her ass against my morning erection, and I wrap my arms around her middle to bring her closer. She shifts in my embrace and brushes her soft lips against mine.

"How did you sleep?" I mutter, threading my fingers into her hair.

Aurelia nods, rubbing her nose against mine. She rolls me onto my back, kissing the skin of my chest as she moves with me, nipping at the scars at my ribs. She throws a leg over my lap, and I grab her hips, grinding her naked center against my dick. She's warm and wet, and I'd give anything to have sex with my wife.

Give anything to have this hell past us for good.

She brushes her tits against my chest, stretching her arms under my pillow as I rub against her heat. Even her kiss is different—not urgent, but hard like she's trying to hurt me.

With a jerk, I break from her lips, pressing my head further into the pillow.

When she sits up, she has a Morganite dagger in her hand, and I freeze.

Was it something I said?

"If you wanted a divorce, you could have just asked," I offer nervously. "No need to get homicidal."

Her gaze pierces me to the bed as she tosses the blade from one hand to the other. That motion claws at my brain, and the pit of dread in my belly grows.

"What's the matter, dear," she says as her eyes grow cold, an odd accent coloring her words. "Don't like a little pain with your pleasure?"

If I didn't know that something was off before, the thick Irish brogue coming from her mouth would've raised a huge fucking red flag.

My whole body goes cold.

I know that accent, that cadence, that sick fucking voice.

This is not my wife.

"Iva? I gotta say, the body's new. Wanna tell me what the fuck you're doing?" I buck her off me, scrambling from the bed as fast as I can.

I'm positive I've never been *less* happy that I'm buck-ass naked.

"Mmm," she purrs on a smirk, her tongue sweeping her upper lip. "I do so love seeing my handiwork on you."

Bile rises in my throat as her eyes roam my body—examining each thick scar she'd carved into my skin. Even though she has Aurelia's face, I want to rip her fucking head off.

"What do you want?" I demand, surreptitiously

searching for something to secure her with before this gets really bad.

So many things could go wrong. And knowing how fucking crazy Iva is...

"I want to take your love from you," she admits, a sick smile curling Aurelia's lips. "I'm going to enjoy making you watch her die."

I save one little life, and it blows my whole world apart. *No good deed goes unpunished.*

"Why? Because I stopped you from murdering an innocent woman? That's not our purpose. It's not our job to judge or change. It is our job to send souls on. Period. The end."

"And who are you to tell me what our purpose is, you impertinent little fledgling?" she snarls, jabbing the air with that deadly blade.

"I became that person when I read the archives," I confess for the first time. "They told me what our role is —the role the head families are keeping secret so you don't kill off their kin. That's the real reason you spelled Lucien, isn't it? He was digging a little too deep? Knew a little too much? Abusing his job title a little too much for your liking?"

She looks almost pleased I've figured out her game. Like I'm a dog that finally figured out how to shit outside. If she weren't wearing Aurelia's face...

"Yes, it was unfortunate Lucien had to die," she simpers, "but making you kill him was just a bonus. It was also a pleasant little perk making Aurelia hate you —taking away what you most wanted. Your girl sure can hold onto a grudge. And now that you have her, I'm going to enjoy making you watch her slit her own throat before you die."

As she reveals her master plan, I notice my jeans at the foot of the bed, my black leather belt still threaded through the loops. Flicking my eyes back to her, I watch as she raises the dagger.

Her movements change from the flowing grace Iva usually possesses, to an uncoordinated jerky shake— the knife trembling in her hand.

My woman is in there, fighting back.

Her face screws up in concentration, sweat popping up on her brow as the battle wages inside my beautiful wife's body. The knife rises again, slowly heading for her slender, perfect neck.

Wasting no time, I snatch the belt from the loops, roughly ripping the knife from her clenched fingers, and binding her wrists with the leather. I shove her face in the duvet as she struggles against the bonds.

I don't bother to dress—I just yell for Evan.

She pops in a moment later, fully phased and snarling. Well, until she sees me buck-ass naked.

"Are you kidding me with this?" she shrieks, covering her eyes. "I'm blind! West is going to kick your ass."

None of this is funny, and despite Evan's dramatics, there are worse problems than her seeing me naked.

"It's Iva, Evan. She's stowed away in Aurelia's brain. You mind taking over here so I can put some fucking pants on?"

"You got it," she shudders, mumbling under her breath that it's like seeing her brother naked as she takes Iva's bonds in her hands.

I throw on my jeans and rip the sheet off the bed to cover my woman.

"Now what?" Evan asks, struggling to hold onto Aurelia's restraints.

I have no fucking clue.

AURELIA

Realizing I'm chained to the bed is not on my list of top-five favorite ways to wake up. I'm a little fuzzy on the details, but I'm pretty sure I didn't sign on for this particular kink.

At least I have clothes on. What the hell happened last night?

I tug on the chain, the links rattling against the

wood of the bed frame and rousing Rhys from a fitful sleep. Relegated to the bedside chair, he's barefoot and scruffy, wearing rumpled jeans and a wrinkled T-shirt.

"Umm." I chuckle nervously. "I think I was supposed to pick a safe word before the bonds came into play. Wanna tell me what's going on?"

"Sure," he replies, his voice rough with sleep, "if you can answer one question. What's your favorite weapon?"

"That depends," I say with a half-shrug, the links clanging against the frame with the movement.

"On?" he asks warily, sitting forward in the chair.

"The situation. If I'm going silent, then my hatchets. If I don't care about noise, a Glock 19. If I want to look pretty, a wakizashi because I'm too short for katanas. If I need silence and distance, I prefer throwing knives."

He breathes out a sigh of relief. "Thank the Fates. You're you."

He rips a hand through his hair, tugging on the strands while he studies my face. The hair-ripping thing is a common tick for him when he's stressed.

"Who the fuck else would I be?" I ask, affronted. But the truth of it slaps me in the face.

I've been losing time. A few seconds at first, and then more. I thought I'd just been spacing out, but...

"Iva must have done something to you, Gorgeous,"

he murmurs, dropping that particular bomb in my lap. "She took over for a little while."

"What do you mean she took over?" I ask, trying unsuccessfully to sit up, my whole body turning to ice. "What did she do?"

The chains aren't too tight, but they aren't loose, either. I'm stuck flat on my back, and the longer he hesitates to tell me what happened, the more I figure just how bad it could have been.

"She attempted to slit your throat," he mutters, his voice gruff and choked. "While I watched."

It's so much worse than I thought.

"You've woken a few times," he rasps, "but she...but she comes through pretty quick."

My brain seems to be stuck on a loop. I keep hearing his broken, hoarse voice say "slit your throat" over and over. I yank on my bonds, knowing I'm not going anywhere, but my limbs are aching to take flight.

"How long have I been like this?"

"Three days," he croaks, raking a hand down his cheek.

Shock makes my body go numb, my mind blank. And then the tears come—great racking sobs ripping through my chest.

She has held me hostage for three fucking days—

invaded my mind, my body. Who knows how long she's been squatting in my brain?

The bitch tortured my husband. Again.

Now I'm helpless—*chained*. A monster has taken me over.

"I really want to hug you, Gorgeous. But the last time I did, she bit me in the neck and tore a sizable chunk out before Evan stopped her."

It takes several minutes for the tears to stop, and even longer for the shaking breaths to cease. In that time, I steel myself, shutting off my emotions, shutting my heart down.

Turning myself to stone.

My voice is still hoarse, but my words are steady.

"You need to find someone to remove the binding," I order with a resigned nod. "Remove it, and leave me here. A better plan would be to kill me, but I won't ask that of you. You need to get as far away from me as you can—as fast as you can. She will never stop. She'll keep hunting you."

It doesn't matter if I'm dead. Iva will hunt him to the ends of the earth, chasing him until she's had her bloodthirsty fill.

His face mottles red before he starts yelling, "I'm *not* giving up on you. We are in this together. I'm not going to let you quit now."

But I'm exhausted—mentally and physically. I don't know if I can go on much longer.

He continues to tell me other things—things I can't understand—because the longer he talks, the more his voice starts to garble. I take one last look at him, knowing this may be the last time I get to see his beautiful face.

Knowing that at any second, Iva could take over.

Knowing I could lose hold of myself at any moment.

A forever without Lucien seemed so long, but I know now that the ache of losing Rhys will haunt me even into the next life.

Losing Rhys will haunt me for eternity.

RHYS

I'm still shouting at my unconscious wife when West busts in the room, kicking in the door with his massive boot. The door has practically split in two, and if Aurelia wakes up, she's going to rip him a new one.

When. Not *if.* Never if.

I rack my brain for any solution that makes sense. We've exhausted all my witch contacts. None of them can protect her. All these years when I was exhausting my favor from the king— making sure she was safe and hidden—she was hiding herself.

Somehow, we have to get her Aegis back. She must be able to use her power to protect herself—there's just no other way.

"We've got a huge fucking problem," West growls, adjusting his grip on the katana in his hand.

He looks like John Rambo and Paul Bunyan had a tattooed baby. Two bandoliers crisscross his red flannel shirt like a gunslinger, a backup katana peeks over his shoulder, and a gun rests at both hips.

I notice all this, but it's in the periphery, the world around me scratching at my brain. All I can think of is the last words Aurelia said to me before she passed out.

She's right. Iva won't stop.

But neither will I.

"Yeah? Add it to the list we have already," I yell as my hands rip through my hair. "I've got bigger problems right now. She wants to dissolve the bond. She wants us to fucking leave her here. She wants to die to save us."

I'm ready to yank it out by the roots. I know she wants us safe—wants the best for me and the rest of us —but Fates be damned, I want her. I refuse to give up on Aurelia just because Iva has a grudge.

No, we're doing this together.

"Well, she's not going to have to save us," he informs me, adjusting his grip on the blade in his hand.

"We're going to have to save ourselves. We're surrounded."

Well, of course we are, I think. *What else can go wrong?*

And then the power goes out.

I had to ask.

19

AURELIA

The blackness fades to gray and then to white. When my eyes finally focus, I realize I'm looking at a white dress. I'd know those skinny-ass hips anywhere.

"Do you like your accommodations?" Iva's Irish brogue stabs through my brain.

I hate that voice.

Given I'm chained to another slab in another gray room when my real body's somewhere else, not so much. She smiles for a second, and suddenly, the bonds are gone. The room seems to melt like candle wax, and now I'm standing on my own two feet in a dimly lit ballroom. The ceiling is vaulted, with a delicate crystal chandelier casting an ethereal glow.

Iva's holding a glass of champagne, gently swaying to a smooth Jazz number on the parquet floor. Her dress is backless and form-fitting, her hair arranged in a neat chignon. Her blood-red lips pull into a smug smile.

"Neat trick." *Bitch.* "Wanna tell me how I got here?"

"You aren't anywhere," she answers with a shrug, still swaying to the music. "You and I are inside your precious little noggin."

I fucking *hate* Jazz, but somehow, I'd be willing to bet she knows that already.

"In my head? I'll buy that. How long have you been squatting inside my brain, you soulless little bitch?"

Her eyebrows rise at the insult, but she seems to let it go. I guess she's having too much fun.

"Well, for the longest time it was impossible to find you," she admits before sipping her drink. "I'd thought I had eliminated all of your kind, but you, darling, you slipped past me. Very tricky, my dear." She raises her glass in a snide mock-toast. "I'd venture a guess Nicola was behind that little coup. Don't you worry. I'll take care of her later."

Iva sashays to a table that seems to have appeared from thin air. Carefully, she peruses the selection of hors d'oeuvres before plucking a canapé from the tray and popping it into her mouth. After taking a fucking age to chew, she shifts to face me.

"I tried finding your Rhys, but he was hidden as well. I blame that infernal Wraith King for that. And then we used your blood. Well, you shed a bit of that for Javier, didn't you? And after I suppressed your Aegis, it was a simple thing to crack your head wide open."

Suppressed not eliminated.

Either she's lying, or Iva has just fucked up.

"Since you're probably going to kill me, could you tell me why? Is it just to secure your throne? For revenge? Or are you just a psychotic bitch on wheels with a God complex? Really, what exactly do you get out of all this?"

For the longest time, I don't think she's going to answer me. Then, she sips from her glass and gently rests the flute on the table. Next to the glass is a sharp-as-sin Morganite knife. She lovingly caresses the blade before wrapping her slender fingers around the hilt, gently picking up the weapon.

"It's a bit of all three, really. But what do I get?" she whispers menacingly as her red lips twist into a cruel smirk. "I get to kill you. I get to rip your mind apart bit by bit, thought by thought, inch by tiny inch."

RHYS

I'm lucky I have friends who can focus during a crisis. While I've been ripping my hair out at Aurelia's bedside, my friends have been raiding her house for weapons.

My wife has weapons tucked away in every nook and cranny of this house. There are knives and handguns inside cabinets disguised as floating shelves, a gun safe hidden behind a wall mirror near the garage door. Every table and bar stool has some kind of weapon affixed to the underside, and that doesn't even include the huge weapons cache hidden in the dojo.

She's like a survivalist or something. If I found a horde of foodstuffs down there, I wouldn't have been surprised. She was prepared—that's for certain. I just wish we'd thought ahead before her mind started to deteriorate.

We should have moved once we realized Aurelia's mind wasn't safe. I should have thought of that. I should have thought of many things—should have anticipated the danger lurking just around the corner.

I should never have left her alone to guard Aidan. Aidan feels it, too—the guilt that she was captured while she watched over him.

And that's where it all went downhill, isn't it?

The house where I lived the best hours of my life is also a place I hate to the very depths of my soul.

I should have realized Javier was a threat. We should have left that house as soon as the first sign of danger skittered down my spine.

Some soldier I turned out to be.

Evan and West drop weapons in a pile just inside the bedroom door, eyeing me warily. After West kicked the door in and the house went black, I may have gone a little batshit.

Okay, that's an understatement.

I turned into a feral, territorial mate and phased—full wingspan, fire, the whole bit. Aurelia is going to need a few new lamps.

And maybe a new mirror.

Her rug is toast, too.

She's going to kick my ass if she wakes up. *When.* When she wakes up.

I managed to tamp down my fire, but the wings seem to be here to stay. Doesn't matter.

I fight better with them, anyway.

My wings are different from Aurelia's. As a soldier, they should match my oracle's, but because of the forced bond, mine are an entirely different color. Whereas Aurelia's fade from blood-red to orange, mine gradually fade from coal-black to burgundy. Though mine are clipped as well, they were cut while I was being tortured prior to the bonding.

That was the only part of her pain I did not feel.

Other than that...I remember every drop of blood spilled.

Every cut.

Every slice.

Iva deserves to pay. She deserves our revenge.

Not only because she tortured my mate—no—but for what she has done to our kind. And for waging this war within our own Legion.

Our people deserve vengeance, too.

And they will have it, I think as I snatch up a Morganite kukri, testing the blade in my grip.

Evan eases into my line of sight again, and her wary expression is almost comical on her fully phased face. Her eyes have bled to black, her talons curled around a gold inlayed sword.

She doesn't try to speak around her fangs because I've heard her try, and that is one sure fire way to get me to laugh my ass off. She sounded like a metal-mouthed teenager with a lisp.

West comes up behind her, his arms encircling her shoulders as he kisses her temple. When he raises his gaze to mine, I know...

That the battle is about to start.

That we're surrounded.

That we probably won't make it out of here alive.

Or at least Aurelia and I won't. I pivot from his hard stare and go back to Aurelia. Leaning over her, my fists sink into the mattress as I press a kiss to her temple.

Her brows furrow even in her fitful slumber, and I close my eyes, breathing in her scent. For the briefest of moments, I let my forehead touch hers before snapping back to standing.

I'll keep them alive.

I'll keep her alive.

Assuming my place just outside the bedroom door, I shield Aurelia as best I can. Evan and West take the second floor with Ian and Aidan as backup. The brothers stick to the shadows, ready to take out any threat that slips past us.

Just keep breathing.

Keep. Breathing.

And with that last thought, soldiers begin storming Aurelia's house, trying to find a breach point.

AURELIA

Her first strike is a tease—a silly feint I easily avoid. The real blow comes when I move to the left, directly into her waiting blade. She makes a shallow slash to the skin of my bicep.

Rooky mistake. I should know better.

As much as it goads me, I have to treat her with the respect she deserves—the cow *did* take over my mind and body.

If I underestimate her, I'm dead.

It's easy to phase here in this dark corner of my brain, the fabric of reality thin. One second, I'm normal, and the next I'm battle-ready. The flames start at my fingertips, catching like a brushfire over the skin of my arms and chest, before coating the skirt of the black dress I only now notice I'm wearing.

What is with this woman and evening dresses? I know I didn't dream this stupid-ass frock on myself.

The wings come next, erupting from my back, and a satisfied smile graces my lips when I hear the fabric of the fancy dress rip. I shudder in relief as the wings fully extend, their blunted tips reaching out to my sides before folding back to resting.

Resting but ready.

I remember so clearly how much I wanted vengeance for Lucien. For my child.

But now, I want it more for myself.

For the life I could have had—with or without Lucien.

For Rhys whose only crime was doing the right thing.

For the wraiths that died in their beds, committing no crime other than being born.

For every Aegis slaughtered.

Testing how the weight affects my balance, I crack my neck and pop my knuckles.

Iva wants my A-game? She'll get it.

Patiently, I wait for her next strike. The whispers of her thoughts buzz like a swarm of wasps, offering me the knowledge she's trying to hide. Strangely, I sense my body on the outside, lying in bed, and here on the inside, coated in the warm fingers of my fire.

How is that possible?

Somehow, I realize if she hurts me here, it will hurt me out there. If she manages to kill me here, I'll be nothing but ashes.

She can't come at me in the real world, so she had to take the coward's way in?

Fuck. That.

Bring it, you fucking hag.

Iva's attack finally comes, but I'm not there. She doesn't appreciate me turning her game on her. She growls at my ingenuity, her perfectly painted lips screwing up as she snarls.

Who's the cat and who's the mouse now, bitch?

Her next assault is interrupted by my fist in her stomach, earning me a gasped groan in response. Before she can retaliate, I've flitted off again, waiting for her next move. She gags at the blow to her stomach before staggering back to standing.

Oh, she's pissed off now, and her Fireskin *whooshes* over her body faster than I can blink.

Aww. I think I made her mad, I think as I chuckle.

And then my chuckle dies.

Slowly, her wings erupt from her back, their mangled form wrenching a gasp from my lips.

Tattered feathers black as her soul, have fallen away in huge patches revealing the raw, red, and bleeding skin underneath.

And then it all becomes clear.

She's dying.

Then the other puzzle pieces in my brain click together.

If there is no one to send you to Hell, then where do you go?

You go nowhere.

20

RHYS

THE STEEL STORM SHUTTERS ON AURELIA'S HOUSE ARE something out of a zombie movie.

Evan used the generator in the basement to trigger the failsafe, slamming them shut before soldiers breached the main entrance. But the attic window was missed, and now they've found a way into the house.

They've breached our walls—the battle has begun.

I'm guarding Aurelia's bedroom, praying no one gets past me. Bodies are piled on the dark hardwood floor, scarlet blood pooling under their bulk. My blades are coated in the gore of the fallen. I use my wings to brush off an attacker, and as he flies into the sheetrock, another approaches from my left. His blade's drawn, ready to cut me down like an errant weed, when my dagger breaches the unfortunate gap in the plates of his body armor.

Four soldiers have met the end of my blade before I'm met with real resistance. The phoenix before me is a big bastard, but unlike so many of them, he actually knows what he's doing.

Taking him down won't be as easy.

West and Evan are paired back-to-back, moving to the living room after being herded down the stairs. He goes high as she goes low, spinning and slicing, smoking out and back again, moving as one. Plucking the life from soldier after soldier, they move in tandem as if they'd been fighting together all their lives.

Ian and Aiden stay to the periphery, exterminating any that get past the three of us. Aidan pops in and out of the shadows, slaying soldiers as he passes, while Ian lies in wait in the gloom.

Although we've only fought together in one battle, I miss Aurelia's presence at my back. Especially when a big motherfucker gets a hit in. The hiss of pain that leaves my mouth is not by my consent.

An agonizing sting rends through my shoulder, the familiar bite of Morganite ricocheting through the limb.

Bastards.

Now I'm pissed. I parry my blade against his as he goes for my head, catching him in the throat with my dagger. Twisting the knife, I open his gullet before ripping out my blade and moving onto the next one.

And the next one.

Cutting them all down until I meet one I can't.

I'm dead—*we're dead*—I know it.

My left arm is useless, hanging listlessly at my side. The soldier in front of me has bested every strike and parry, every feint and backhand.

Everything.

He raises his blade, and I realize my defeat. Slipping my eyes closed, I pray someone sends us on. I pray that when Aurelia and I are reborn, we start again.

That we do it better—be smarter—with less hate and more love. I don't regret a second, because if one thing is certain, she is my Heaven.

She is my peace.

And if I get nothing else, I will know my Heaven is out there somewhere.

And I'll find it.

AURELIA

Even in my subconscious, Rhys' cry of agony reaches me. Stuck in my mind like a fly in sap, pinned in this

Hell with a psychopath, his pain tugs at my soul. The skin of my shoulder splits, blood running the length of my arm as my heart nearly shrivels in my chest.

Oh, no.

I've had about enough of this shit. I've got somewhere to be.

Iva's not as composed as she was before—her hair disheveled and falling from her chignon. Her lipstick is smeared, bleeding into the skin of her cheek.

She comes for me again, but with renewed vigor, slashing and stabbing wildly. But she's making mistakes.

Mistakes she shouldn't with someone like me.

Someone who can kill her.

If she's in my head, I know I'm in hers, too. If I kill her here, maybe, just maybe it will kill her in the real world.

Stepping to the side, I barely miss a wild slash, before reaching up and latching onto her hair—wrenching her head as I sweep her legs out from under her.

Her blade goes flying, shattering into five smaller pieces, skittering across the parquet floor. I use the distraction to flip her body over and smash her pretty little face into the ground. Satisfaction fills me at the sound of her pert nose crunching against the floor.

Scrambling off her back, I tag a shard of the broken blade as Iva staggers her way back to standing.

The front of her white dress is liberally splashed with the crimson running from her nose and mouth. She spits, teeth and blood hitting the floor, and I can't help the gleeful smile that stretches across my face.

Shrieking, she races for me, fingers descended into blunted claws, broken teeth bared. Her scream is cut off to a gurgle as the shard in my hand slides through the smooth skin of her throat.

Bet she didn't see that coming.

Her eyes widen as her lifeblood leeches from her body, running down her chest, soaking into her dress, and pooling onto the floor of my mind. She staggers, collapsing to her back.

She gurgles a gasp once, twice, and then stills.

She's not breathing, but I don't trust it. To be sure, I take the sliver of Morganite in my hand and saw through the remainder of her throat. Undeterred by tissue and bone, I take her head. The jagged, double edge slices into the flesh of my hand, but I don't care.

I'll wear those scars with honor.

RHYS

I wait for a strike that never comes. When I open my eyes, the soldier—who only moments before was ready to take my life—stares, dumbfounded, at the blade as if he has no idea how it got there. The remaining soldiers —at least the ones still standing—have similar expressions on their faces.

It's as if a veil has been lifted, and now they see the truth.

I wonder how many minds Iva controlled to do her bidding. How many poor souls were used to perpetuate a war that no one wanted? It makes me sorry we killed them true dead, but the good ones we'll send on.

And the rest? Good fucking riddance.

Scanning the crowd of confused soldiers, I spot a blood-spattered Evan hugging an equally bloody West. Both seem a little banged up, but no permanent damage. They're all over each other, so I think the relationship cat is out of the bag. Not that it was a surprise to anyone. It was the worst-kept secret in the Black compound.

Neither Ian nor Aidan are within my line of sight, but Ian's booming laugh echoes from the third floor.

A loud clank of a chain sounds from behind me, and

the best voice in the whole world starts cussing a blue streak.

"Hello? Ding, dong the bitch is dead, but I've gotta pee! Can a girl get a fucking rescue here?"

That's my girl.

I try to reach across my body to pull the key from my pocket, but it's not really working out.

"A little help?" I ask Evan.

Evan glances at my pocket, then at the territorial West. Shaking her head, she grabs Aurelia's chain, snapping it from the steel subframe with a tiny flick of her fingers.

Well, that's one way to do it.

"Thank the *Fates*." Aurelia sighs as she hightails it to the bathroom, dragging the chain behind her, brushing a quick peck on my cheek on her way out.

She returns a few minutes later looking relieved, even though she's wounded—her left arm a matching bloody mess to mine. We both need stitches, but I can't bring myself to care.

I should ask what happened—it's plain to see that two battles were fought. But I don't care about anything other than kissing my woman.

Reaching out with my good hand, I sift my fingers under her thick mane, hauling her lips to mine, tasting the mint of freshly brushed teeth.

I pull my head back, raising my brows in question.

"What? I multitasked," she protests. "I didn't want to kiss you with three days' worth of funk on my breath. I'm *considerate*, dammit."

"Did you hide your spitting, too?" I joke, needling her just because I can.

"Shaddup," she says as she sweeps her lips against mine, effectively shutting my mouth.

This is what Heaven feels like—my wife in my arms and a wide-open future that no one can steal from us.

But first we need to make sure the bitch is true dead. For real this time.

AURELIA

The raid on the Legion house in Oregon happened as soon as we could make it on a plane without causing a stir. Something about the woman I'd left behind called to me, and I couldn't leave her there to rot one more second than I had to.

Rhys and I got our wounds treated, everyone got a shower, and off we went. I forgot just how much I hate stitches.

There was no resistance at the gate—even with two exiles and four wraiths in tow. The soldiers practically waved us in.

The house buzzed with whispers—more because of the reappearance of Nicola than from our appearance at the gate. Apparently, Nicola had been cast out over a month ago when the gentry were recalled from their posts. But in the few short hours it took us to get there, and with no one able to find Iva, Nicola had taken up the position of Primary.

No one questioned it—the air of relief palpable with each passing minute Iva remained gone.

In a cell or not, these people had been prisoners, too.

It takes hours searching all the rooms in the prisoner hallway, but we still can't find Iva's remains or the woman my conscience is screaming at me to save.

I can't put my finger on it, but something about her is clawing at my mind. Since my mind has been clawed enough, I need to know she's all right.

From what we gathered from the residents, Iva killed most of the prisoners before soldiers were sent to kill us. Their ashes were sent back to their families in a macabre show of power, but their souls were gone.

Irritated at the lack of help or answers, I finally break down and ask Nicola where Iva's personal quarters are located. She's happy to oblige, as long as I say please.

Fates give me patience. Because if you give me strength, I'm going to kill this bitch.

"Please," I grind out, and she accepts my half-assed gesture.

She leads us to the third floor inside an opulent bedroom. All along the east wall are enormous built-in bookcases. Some of the columns are filled with books, but many—*so many*—of the others are filled with gray canisters.

Moving closer, I realize what I'm looking at.

Glass jars.

Glass jars filled with ashes.

Thick, vibrating energy radiates from them. I know that feeling—I've been missing it since Iva suppressed my Aegis.

And then I finally understand...

This is how she had so much power—why she lived so far past the norm for our species.

This is why the Aegis were being slaughtered.

Horror brings bile up my throat.

How many lives is she responsible for? I wonder, trying and failing to count the jars displayed like trophies.

"Hey, come look at this," Ian calls from the other side of the room.

On the wide, king-size sleigh bed are remnants of ashes on the duvet and sheets, but it looks as if someone has hastily scrapped them off the fabric.

Dread sours the feeling of triumph in my belly.

Too easy. All of this was too easy.

Who knows what kind of nut job could have those ashes? And given the number of jars in this room, we might never find her. Those ashes could be anywhere.

My worry practically grows a new head as the realization, that until a wraith sends her to Hell, someone could bring her back.

It takes days to send each of the Aegis souls on. We go through every single jar, the final count over two thousand. Only fifty of those souls were handed over to the wraiths to consume.

Fifty that were evil out of two thousand souls. My mind still refuses to make sense of the carnage.

After we go through the jars on the shelves, we raid every nook and cranny of Iva's room, coming up empty. I plop down on a fragile settee—secretly hoping I break it—and catch a faint noise near my left ear. I stop moving and shush the room, silently waiting for the sound again.

There.

Beyond the thick material on the north wall, a weak moan escapes the tapestry. No one else seems to hear it, but I know someone is behind that wall. West and Rhys work together, ripping the curtain from its rungs to reveal a small wooden door.

West steps back and kicks it in with his wide, heavy boot. The stench wafting from the depths of the black room speaks of death and blood and torture.

Rhys lights up his right hand and steps close to the ailing body of an emaciated, unconscious girl.

This is her—the girl I've searched this whole house for.

Her dark hair covers her face, and when I pull the matted strands back, my world nearly spins off its axis.

My legs refuse to hold me, and I crash to my knees.

"What is it, Gorgeous?" Rhys asks.

But he couldn't know.

Only someone as close as we once were would recognize her now.

"That's Mena," I say on a gasping sob. "That's my sister."

Thank you so much for reading Flame Kissed. I can't express just how much I love Aurelia & Rhys. And we aren't quite done yet! Next up is Mena & Asher and all the heartbreaking, forbidden fated mates chaos that is to come.

Death Kissed is next on the menu, and I hope you're buckled in to see the damaged, formerly-caged Phoenix and her swoony, over-protective Wraith mate.

GET IT NOW!

Want the skinny on future releases without having to follow me absolutely everywhere on social media?
Text "LEGION" to (844) 311-5791

I'm the last one of my kind. He's sentenced to death.

After fifty years in a squalid cell, I'm finally free. Problem is, everything I had is long gone, and the sister I shunned in my youth is now my savior.

But seeing him next to my hospital bed makes me forget that my touch is deadly. Or maybe Asher has a death wish of his own.

***Because my powers are coming back, and they
could burn us all.***

ASHER

I'm running out of time.

I think this as I watch my King gripping the handrail
as he shakily makes his way down the stairs to the
subbasement medical bay. His white knuckles clutch
the banister, and I realize he's weaker today than he
was yesterday. He's fading fast.

Too fast.

I feel like an asshole for thinking it, but the further
John's health deteriorates, the more I know I'm a
dead man.

Gods, I'm a selfish prick.

Here I thought I'd get to die in battle or maybe after
I got to watch my children and grandchildren grow up.
But that won't happen. I don't get a mate or children. I
wasted too much time on my job, and now I get to
watch the man I've considered the closest thing I have
to a father wither away to nothing. I get to see my life
and my future shrivel to a husk and blow away in the
wind.

The job I put so much of myself in will kill me as
soon as he takes his last breath.

And there's nothing I can do about it. No foe to fight, no sword to clash.

Wraiths are a tricky bunch. So many of our kind are two-faced assholes. Hiding. Scheming. Manipulative.

When you're the gatekeeper to Hell, sometimes the honor system shits the bed a bit.

But the one thing we're completely transparent about is our mate. John is dying because his mate Olivia is—plain and simple. When a wraith mates, it is a life-long commitment, effectively wrapping two souls with the same thread of life. If one goes, so does the other, and Olivia has been sick—so sick her guardians are scrambling to find a cure for what ails her. Scrambling to save her and their hides as well.

The longer it lasts, the more I know they won't find some magical remedy to knock Olivia off the path she's on. When a guardian's charge dies, the guardian must forfeit their life for failing to save them.

That's the oath we take—an oath we pay for in blood.

I've never regretted taking the vow to serve John, never wanted to change the path of my life, never wanted to be anything else once I was cast out of what was left of my family after my parents' shameful turn.

But now as I look death in the face, I wish I'd lived more, done more, seen more.

Regret, thy name is Asher.

John reaches the med bay and pauses before he opens the heavy steel door. He turns to level his chocolate-brown eyes at me and my hulking dipshit of a cousin standing just to my left.

"I need you two to stay sharp in there. Aurelia says her sister is a full-blown Aegis. And from what I gather, she is remarkably and understandably unstable. Do not touch her. If you think she is about to lose it, you leave the room. Do your best to avoid engagement. She has been locked away as Iva's personal punching bag for the last fifty years. You know how much that woman was a fan of torture."

I hold in my shudder at the thought of someone being in that crazy bitch's clutches for fifty years. I don't care if it seems emasculating, that woman scares the shit out of me. I don't care if she's ashes, phoenixes have a way of coming back. Trusting that Iva is even remotely dead, seems just plain stupid in my book.

"What are they doing here?" Cam growls at our king. "We just got Aurelia's trouble-bringing ass out of our lives, and now she's back? With a sister? Are you kidding me?"

Fucking imbecile.

Cam hasn't always been too bright. As a teenager, he believed all of his parents' hateful rhetoric.

Phoenixes are evil. They oppress wraiths. They kill us. And while some of that is true on some levels, phoenixes aren't the only ones who despise what we are, and not all of them do. Every single faction of the Ethereal has their share of members who hate or fear us. As they should. If they fuck up, we're the ones to send them packing straight to Hell when they die.

Cam used to be reasonable, after getting out from under his odious parents. But since their deaths, especially since it was on Iva's orders, hate fills him.

The longer he stews in this horrible malevolence, the more I worry about him turning into a Revenant.

Turning isn't too hard to do. Most wraiths are half out of our minds, anyway. Consuming enough evil to keep us alive can easily taint the soul. Even the most honorable wraith just needs one little push—a paltry little shove—and bloodlust takes over. Clouding our mind, our souls, taking the need to consume evil just that tiny step further, and then we're not just taking in evil souls, we're eating the flesh of the corrupt.

When I shake out of my thoughts, John's silence stretches and grows until his once-brown eyes turn black. His stare seems to shrink my fuckup of a cousin until it's clear by the expression on Cam's face that he feels three feet tall.

"Do we need to have this discussion again?" John's

low voice grates in the small space. "We owe her. We owe the *both* of them. A snake was in our midst, and we saw nothing. They took out Javier and Iva. Aurelia's vision saved us all. They defended this house and your King when they could have run. They fought in your stead to save your life. Show them some fucking respect."

It doesn't matter that he is weak. It doesn't matter that his once-dark hair is turning whiter by the day, heralding his death more than any other sign could. He could give Cam a lesson without moving an inch.

"Yes, sir," Cam mutters, eyes downcast. He fakes contrition, but I know he has zero remorse for his hatred. It's evident by the unyielding line of his shoulders and the fixed set of his jaw. He feels nothing but rage.

Fucking moron, I think as I slap him upside the back of his idiot head once John's back is turned.

Cam flinty blue gaze slices to me, but I refuse to back down. One of these days, I won't hold back when I punch him in the face. He nearly signed his own death warrant just two weeks ago. If I hadn't kept him in line, kicked his ass, and practically held his fucking hand the whole damn time, John would have had his head already. Unstable and malignant, I've slept the fewest hours of my life watching out for him.

One of these days, I won't be here to save his ass.

John grunts as he pushes the door open, but I refrain from helping him. I learned very early on—once he started to deteriorate—that letting him do what he could for himself was the only way either of us were going to survive. The room beyond has stark-white walls and gray cement floors, and while it appears pristine, it carries the faint smell of earth and dirt. I suppose being this far underground will taint the air no matter how many air purifiers are running.

Eight hospital-grade beds—four on each side—line the room. Each bay has the required oxygen ports, IV stands, and monitoring devices. Most of the bays have their privacy curtains open, but one in the far-back right is pulled shut.

Carver is still in the med bay and hasn't yet regained consciousness after a vicious attack from his mate, Javier. At this point, I am not certain it is a bad thing. Javier turned Revenant unbeknownst to us all. A puppet for Iva to infiltrate this house, and now that his mate is dead, I dread the day when we have to tell him what happened. While it doesn't appear as if Carver had any knowledge of Javier's deceit, it is a general rule that most people have a hard time looking at someone who ignored the signs of violence. Mass murder, no matter the cause or reason, usually carries a taint that stains the survivors.

The only other occupied bay has the privacy curtains open, and the rest of the members of the house are loosely surrounding the bed, blocking my view of our newest houseguest.

I still can't believe Aurelia is a twin. I hope they aren't identical, because two of her unpredictable asses would most likely be the worst thing I could think of. The last thing we need in this house is more crazy, yet here we are.

Aidan and Ian block my view, but that doesn't matter. I have no interest in the Psychic Wonder's sister. I just hope her presence is more transitory than it seems. The last thing we need is her to hole up here when everything in our lives is about to change.

And it is. Make no mistake.

If John dies without a plan of succession, we are all fucked.

The brothers move to the side out of John's way, and my King introduces himself to the patient.

"Hello, Mena. My name is John Black. Welcome to my home. I'm happy you are with us, and you made it out of there. You and your family are invited to stay here as long as you need."

Oh, great, just lay down the welcome mat, John.

"Anything you need from us, please just let us know."

Out of the corner of my eye, I see a dark-haired head nod hesitantly. She doesn't make a noise, not a sound, not a whisper. How odd.

Finally, she clears her throat, and then a soft, but hoarse voice speaks. "Th-thank you, sir. Thank you for letting me impose on your generous hospitality. I will not forget this kindness."

That voice.

Something about that voice pulls at me, as if there were steel strings around my soul, and they are finally being reeled home. Without thought, my body moves. I gently push Aidan out of my way so I can get closer. He obliges with a grunt of indignation, but I don't care. He takes forever to move.

Finally.

Finally, I can see her. Her bowed head and downcast eyes are in deference to the king. She's rail thin, the shapeless hospital gown billowing around her like a sail. Her wrists and arms are mottled with purple and green bruises.

And the scars...

Faint pink lines crisscross old white ones up and down both arms. A few of her fingers are irreparably disfigured, especially the pinky finger on her right hand.

It is crooked and curled, and even though the rest of her fingers are moving, picking at the nonexistent pills on her blanket, that one lone pinky remains still. Her fingernails are cracked and jagged but clean and scrubbed.

I taste the metallic tinge of blood on my tongue, and I realize my fangs have descended and have sliced my lip. I feel the pinch of my talons growing from the tips of my fingers, and I understand that my body has gone into a full phase without my mind ever asking it to. Rage, the likes I have never felt, washes through me, and I realize I want to murder someone for the first time in my long life. I've killed in my three hundred years of service to the king, but never have I relished the deaths.

But right this second, I want to know who did this to her. I want to know if it was just Iva or a host of her soldiers. I want to rip the skin and muscle from their bones as they watch. I want to consume them until they are left writhing in the depths of Hell.

My brain seems to split in two. I want to maim and murder, but I also want to comfort her. I can almost taste the bitterness of her distress, how much she must hate people looking at her, talking to her after so many years of captivity. I want to see her eyes. I want to know what she's thinking. I can't take the waiting, and I move

Ian out of the way and then West and then Evan, making my way to the left side of her bed.

I hear faint sounds of protests and shouts beyond the harsh buzzing in my ears, but I don't care. I know my hands are taloned, but I can't think about reining in my phase.

I reach out to touch her fidgeting fingers, and in surprise, her head finally rises so I can see her face. Her eyes are wide and fringed in black lashes that make her beautiful olive-green irises pop. Her forehead and the left side of her face are covered in bruises, and her nose is pert and cute, even if it's a little swollen. Her cheekbones are high and sharp, and as soon as I can, I'm making her eat until she bursts.

Those eyes that only a second ago were startled, swiftly turn from surprised to angry, and in a flash, her irises turn from green to gold.

The last thought of consciousness I have before she shocks me stupid is how pretty her eyes are when she's mad.

Grab Death Kissed today!

BOOKS BY ANNIE ANDERSON

SEVERED FLAMES

Ruined Wings

IMMORTAL VICES & VIRTUES

HER MONSTROUS MATES

Bury Me

SHADOW SHIFTER BONDS

Shadow Me

THE ARCANE SOULS WORLD

GRAVE TALKER SERIES

Dead to Me

Dead & Gone

Dead Calm

Dead Shift

Dead Ahead

Dead Wrong

Dead & Buried

SOUL READER SERIES

Night Watch

Death Watch

Grave Watch

THE WRONG WITCH SERIES

Spells & Slip-ups

Magic & Mayhem

Errors & Exorcisms

THE LOST WITCH SERIES

Curses & Chaos

Hexes & Hijinx

THE ETHEREAL WORLD

PHOENIX RISING SERIES

(Formerly the Ashes to Ashes Series)

Flame Kissed

Death Kissed

Fate Kissed

Shade Kissed

Sight Kissed

To stay up to date on all things Annie Anderson, get exclusive access to ARCs and giveaways, and be a member of a fun, positive, drama-free space, join The Legion!

facebook.com/groups/ThePhoenixLegion

ACKNOWLEDGMENTS

A huge, honking thank you to Shawn, Barb, Jade, Angela, Heather, Kelly, and Erin. Thanks for the late-night calls, the endurance of my whining, the incessant plotting sessions, the wine runs... (*looking at you, Shawn.*)

Every single one of you rock and I couldn't have done it without you.

ABOUT THE AUTHOR

Annie Anderson is the author of the international best-selling Rogue Ethereal series. A United States Air Force veteran, Annie pens fast-paced Urban Fantasy novels filled with strong, snarky heroines and a boatload of magic. When she takes a break from writing, she can be found binge-watching The Magicians, flirting with her husband, wrangling children, or bribing her cantankerous dog to go on a walk.

To find out more about Annie and her books, visit www.annieande.com

facebook.com/AuthorAnnieAnderson

instagram.com/AnnieAnde

amazon.com/author/annieande

bookbub.com/authors/annie-anderson

goodreads.com/AnnieAnde

pinterest.com/annieande

tiktok.com/@authorannieanderson

www.ingramcontent.com/pod-product-compliance
Lightning Source LLC
Chambersburg PA
CBHW061318190726
48288CB00002B/553